YOUNG HEROES

GOLD RUSH!

John L. Jenkins
Mark W. Weaver

MARY MUHLENBERG is an ambitious sixteen-year-old who joins the California Gold Rush in 1849. But unlike her missionary parents, she exchanges her Bible for a spade. Mary longs for a better life, despite her own conscience and her father's warnings.

Touched by gold fever, Mary makes an ill-advised alliance with conniving entrepreneurs from Midas, a nearby mining town. Rejecting both her father and the timely advice of a wise and respected Californio, she will not abandon her chosen path. Mary's escapades will threaten her father's work among the Feather River tribes, compromise her faith and family, and ultimately imperil not only her life, but the lives of her friends.

Mary finally comes face to face with her shortcomings, but evil plans beyond her control are already in motion. Trapped and alone, Mary must confront the darkness within herself. Only then will she be ready for the greatest test of her life, with the lives of others hanging in the balance.

Midas Touch, Book 1

STORYSHOPUSA.COM

MANASSAS, VIRGINIA

Gold Rush!
John Jenkins, Mark Weaver

storyshopusa.com

Published by Story Shop USA, Manassas, Virginia 20110.

Cover design: Story Shop USA
Front cover and interior drawings: Steven Philip Morales
Gold Rush Map: Mark Weaver

Library of Congress Control Number: TB

AUTHOR'S NOTE

Saturday, January 24, 1998, marked the launch of the California Gold Discovery to Statehood Sesquicentennial program. This 33-month long program celebrated the 150th anniversaries of the discovery of gold at Sutter's Mill in 1848, the ensuing Gold Rush of 1849, and the initiation of California's statehood in 1850. In those original 33 months between 1848 and 1850, over 50,000 Americans made their way west by land or sea or both, facing deprivation, disease and death. The equivalent percentage of today's population would be a half million Americans—risking their lives, their families and their futures in a quest for instant wealth.

Now, more than 150 years later, the California Gold Rush continues to yield valuable insights into the fabric of our nation, past and present. Of all the lessons that can be learned from a cursory visit to that tumultuous pioneering period in American history, one lesson stands out above all the rest: we did not learn our lessons!

In *Gold Rush!*, we snatch you from your 21st century surroundings and deposit you into the bottom of a ravine in the summer heyday of 1849, among the rocky hills near the North Fork of the Feather River and the soaring Sierra mountain range. There you begin your visit, kneeling on the rocky soil beneath a clear blue sky. But unlike the characters in this story, you are not infected with the most contagious and deadly disease of that day—not cholera, but as the local Californios would say, la fiebre del oro—gold fever.

And when you and your family have finished your visit with Mary, Solomon and Ignácio, and have returned to the comforts of the present day, stop for a moment, listen to your heart, and ask yourself this question: what lessons can I learn from the California Gold Rush?

GOLD RUSH!

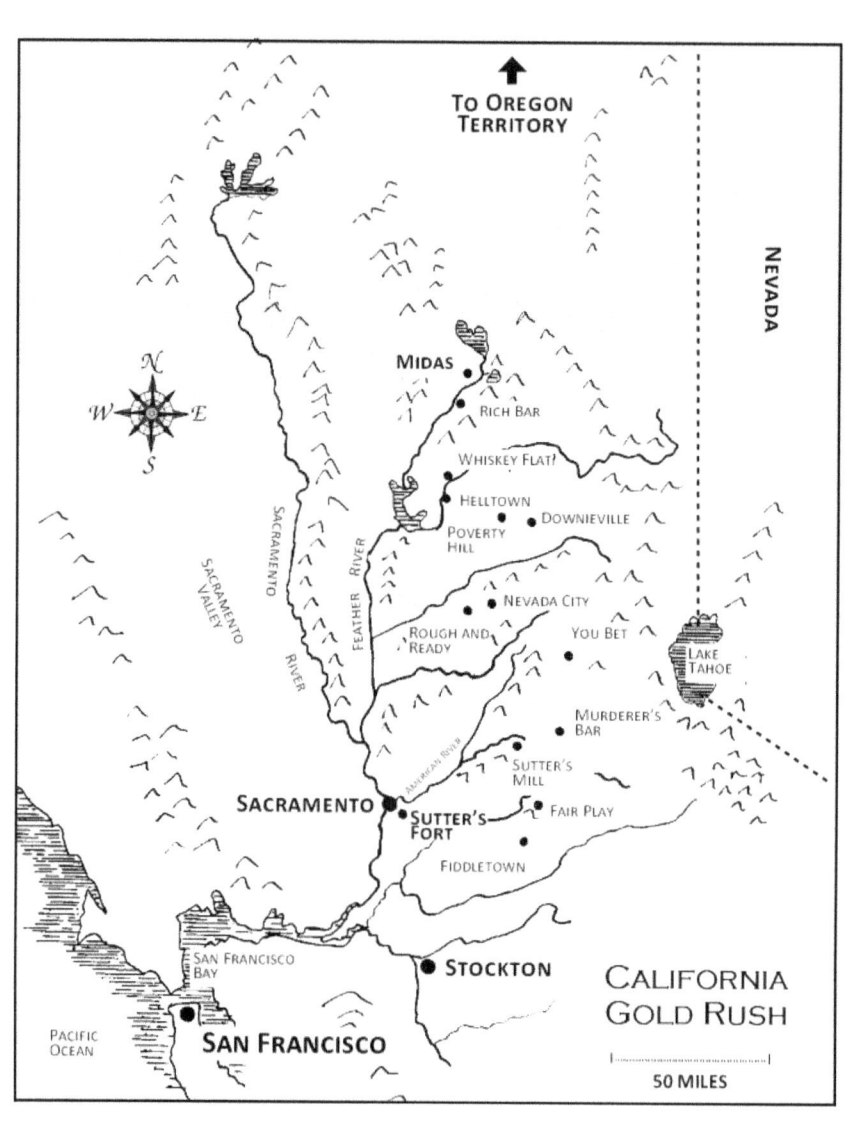

TO OREGON
TERRITORY

NEVADA

N
W E
S

MIDAS

RICH BAR

WHISKEY FLAT!

SACRAMENTO RIVER

FEATHER RIVER

HELLTOWN
POVERTY
HILL

DOWNIEVILLE

SACRAMENTO
VALLEY

NEVADA CITY

ROUGH AND
READY

YOU BET

LAKE
TAHOE

RIVER

MURDERER'S
BAR

AMERICAN RIVER

SUTTER'S
MILL

SACRAMENTO

SUTTER'S
FORT

FAIR PLAY

FIDDLETOWN

SAN FRANCISCO
BAY

STOCKTON

CALIFORNIA
GOLD RUSH

PACIFIC
OCEAN

SAN FRANCISCO

50 MILES

CHAPTER 1

GOLD DIGGER

MARY leaned forward on her knees and tightly gripped her spade with both hands. She angled the blade toward the hard, bluish clay and gravel in front of her.

The sixteen-year-old ignored the stinging streams of sweat dripping from her auburn hair and dusty forehead into her wide-open brown eyes. She ignored the dark shadows of her two friends cast by the noonday sun.

Abruptly, the loud rattling sound filling the narrow ravine halted. She did not hesitate. She plunged the spade downward and pinned the snake to the ground behind its triangular head.

The snake wriggled once, then went limp. To be safe, Mary raised the spade and came down hard a second and a third time.

The two brothers whooped and laughed. Mary grabbed the dead snake with both hands and flung the two pieces into a clump of nearby brush.

"Last time that rattler's gonna mess with our diggin's!" exclaimed Tom Nielsson, who had just turned fifteen. He swung his shovel onto his shoulder.

Billy, a year younger, patted Mary on the back.

"Our diggings . . ." Mary muttered, wiping her hands on her torn corduroy pants.

They had panned the creek beds near the Feather River for

nearly a month. But for what? Hardly two ounces of gold—though they'd started mining the same week she and her missionary parents staggered into the town of Midas. Their journey from Shawnee Mission, Kansas, to northern California took three deadly months. Starting in March, they'd come west with an outfit of eighteen families who called themselves the Kansas Trading Company. They'd ridden and then walked a thousand miles over endless plains, perilous deserts and rugged mountains.

Mary didn't want to think about how many died from accidents, fever, and chills that spring. Of those who survived the journey, only her parents had chosen to live so far north of San Francisco.

She scrunched her sunburned face and blew a tickling wisp of hair away from her freckled nose. Digging and sifting the rocky soil—mining was hard! And when they panned the streambeds, the cold water numbed their fingers. Even on a hot summer day!

She sighed. As her shadow shifted, sunlight struck the blue clay and broken rock where her spade had severed the snake.

A yellow glint caught her eye. Mary drew in a sharp breath. Her heart skipped a beat. Could it really be?

"Tom! Billy! I've found color!"

She rubbed a dirty sleeve across her face to wipe the sweat, then pulled out her knife. Hunkering down, she scraped it along a narrow crevice in the rock. The brothers dropped to their knees and yanked off their hats to get a better look.

Carefully Mary lifted her knife from the crevice. Her mouth hung open, her eyes riveted on the knife and its glittering load.

Balanced on the level blade gleamed a dozen thick, bright flakes of gold.

"El Dorado, at last!" Billy yelled at the top of his lungs.

Mary watched both brothers joyously fling their tattered and dusty hats high into the air. She imagined the Spanish conquistadors would have tossed their shining helmets too, had they ever discovered that legendary city of gold.

"A real honest to goodness lode!" Tom exclaimed.

Mary yanked a leather pouch from her belt and pried it open with her fingers. Then she slowly tipped the knife. The chips of gold fell inside one by one.

They dug the clay-filled crevice most of the afternoon. More than once, they stopped to hoot and marvel. In three hours, they found more gold than many a seasoned miner found in two weeks.

Mary climbed to her feet and brushed the loose dirt from her pants. With a wide smile, she tossed the pouch from one hand to the other. "I'd say we'll split at least a pound, maybe more."

She handed Tom the pouch so he could feel the weight of success.

Tom just shook his head in disbelief, then tossed it to Billy.

"At sixteen dollars and ounce, that's eighty to ninety dollars for each of us," Mary figured out loud as she loosened her long braid of hair.

"What are you gonna do with your share, Mary?" Billy asked.

"I'm not sure," she said, picking up her canteen and pouring water over her upturned face. She shook the water from her thick hair. "This is my first bonanza."

"Ours too!" Tom said, snatching the pouch from Billy. "We've got to stake our claim. Mary, go ahead—you found the pile."

Billy grabbed their axe and handed it to Mary after she finished weaving her hair back into a braid that reached halfway down her back.

Taking the axe, Mary glanced around and found an old stump to the right side of the ravine. She walked over, swung the axe up over her head, and then slammed it down into the stump.

Billy pulled a sharpened piece of charcoal from his pocket and knelt by the stump. He spoke the words proudly as he wrote them on the handle of the axe.

"EL DORADO CLAIM!"

Tom dropped the pouch into Mary's waiting and open palm.

"July 28, 1849—a day we'll all remember," Mary beamed.

"Now, let's go record our claim and find out what our gold is really worth!"

CHAPTER 2

MIDAS

HALFWAY up the long hill to her home, Mary adjusted her pack. She stared down the rocky path to the rushing North Fork of the Feather River. The river roiled madly a hundred feet below. Her gaze followed the purplish-green ribbon of white-crested water less than a half-mile downstream where it widened and calmed as it rounded a series of sandbars. Amber willows and Indian rhubarb that would flame red in autumn lined the river banks. Pine-crested, rocky foothills rose on either side.

Crowding those foothills, sprawled the mining town of Midas, named after the legendary king who could turn anything to gold with a single touch.

On the north side, a single dirt street and two dozen wooden buildings zigzagged up the steep slope. From the middle of the Z rose a three-story hotel called Heaven's Gate. Solomon's Store & Intelligence Office sat downhill to the left. And downhill from the store stood his two-story saloon, The Queen of Sheba.

Across the river, a camp of about eighty canvas tents called Tent Town dotted the hillside. The number of miners changed daily, rising and falling on the latest rumors of gold. Now, as the day ended, weary miners filed home from surrounding hills. Smoke wafted upward from dozens of cooking fires.

Mary turned back up the rocky path. Grinning, she patted the pouch strapped to her belt. Her portion of the three-way split earned her a six-ounce share worth $96. And more importantly, she and Tom and Billy had recorded their claim at Solomon's Store. Now the ravine was theirs, and theirs alone, to mine. A hangman's noose would find the neck of any foolish miner who thought he could dig on someone else's legal claim.

Five minutes later, the path ended at a grassy crest. Mary could see a breathtaking, rose-streaked sky through the wooden frame of her father's half-built church. Beyond the church stood their three-room cabin and animal pen, nestled between a stand of aspen and a stone bluff.

As she neared the church, the cabin door opened and her father stepped outside. He carried a sturdy lantern built to withstand wind and rain.

Peter Muhlenberg stood six feet tall with a strong chin and honest blue eyes. But the exhausting journey west and a near fatal bout with the fever had left him rail thin. His gray hair and clean-shaven face made him seem out of place in Midas. The only men seen in town or around the diggings without some facial hair were men from the various Maidu tribes.

Mary's shoulders sagged. She knew she was late. For the third time this week, her chores would go undone before dinner.

To her surprise, her father's face gave no hint of displeasure. He broke into a smile and hugged her. Before she could think of what to say, he gently grabbed her hand.

"Daughter, come with me!"

He led her back down the grassy crest, stopping beside the path leading to Midas. Then Mary saw the new lamp pole. Coming up the path, she'd somehow missed seeing it.

Peter hung the lantern on the pole arm. He lit the lantern and upped the wick.

"Now we can give light unto all who are in Midas and the surrounding Sierras."

Mary turned her head and glanced at the church's bare wooden frame. No progress had been made in a week and a half.

"Father, your church has no walls, no roof and only three members," she said with a long sigh. "You, mom and me."

"Yes, that's true," Peter said with a half smile, placing his arm around her shoulders. "But it's built on a firm foundation—rock, not sand like Midas."

Mary sighed and slipped out from under her father's arm. "Don't you understand? The miners and townspeople aren't interested in coming to church. Not now, anyway. They're interested in only one thing."

"And, you, what are you interested in?" Peter asked softly. "Your chores go undone. You're behind in your studies. You have yet to help with the church. The animal pens need enlarging. And I hammer in the Midas foundry four days a week to keep food on our table. Need I say more?"

"But Father, just today, I finally found our first lode! How can I work here when the treasure's down there, just for the taking?"

Mary pulled her pouch from her belt. "Look! My share was almost a hundred dollars—I'll give ten to the church! And we recorded our claim! I think there's even more gold where we got this."

Mary raised her hand and pointed east to jagged hills a mile and a half away.

Peter's eyes followed her outstretched hand. "Where exactly did you stake your claim? The Maidu consider several areas near that rock shelf as sacred."

Sacred? Goose bumps tingled up her back. She knew that her father had been seeking out the tribal headmen from the first day they arrived.

She pointed again. "That clump of pines hides the ravine where I found the gold."

Peter sighed deeply. "That's the entrance to a secluded lake and Maidu burial grounds. I'd hoped gold wouldn't be discovered there."

Mary's freckled cheeks turned red. From her father's work among the Shawnee and other Midwestern tribes, she knew how important the sacred areas would be to the Maidu. And she also knew her father was hurt more than his voice revealed.

"You know our mission. I'm bringing the gospel of Christ to the tribes of the Sierras," her father continued soberly. "We must not begin with an offense."

The flush in Mary's cheeks deepened, but not from shame.

"Father, please! It's Tom and Billy's claim too. Everyone will benefit—the church, your mission, our family! The Maidu must know they are losing their homelands to the gold rush."

Peter nodded silently for several moments, then lowered his eyes to meet hers. Mary knew the look.

"Don't forbid me!" she pleaded, her throat tight. "We've sacrificed our whole lives to serve the Shawnee, the Delaware, and the Munsee. And now, the Maidu. We've never had a place of our own and never owned nice things! And what little we owned, we lost clawing our way here."

Mary opened the pouch and dumped several flakes into her hand. The reflecting sun filled her palm with golden light. "Finding this gold—maybe it's God way of showing his favor and blessing us."

Her father's eyes drooped suddenly—whether from weariness or sadness, Mary wasn't sure. For several minutes, he stood by her side, staring down at the now-busy streets of

Midas and the gray curls of smoke rising from Tent Town across the river.

As the last sliver of ruby sun vanished behind the rugged Sierra range, her father finally turned and spoke.

"Perhaps," he said softly, "perhaps. But also remember this: Where your treasure is, there will your heart be also."

CHAPTER 3

CIGARS

Morning sunlight speared into Mary's eight-by-eight room through her makeshift window. The window did not have a glass pane like her bedroom window in Shawnee Mission. Instead of a glass pane, a dozen glass jars were held in place about the necks by clay and stone.

The golden light reflected Mary's smiling face in the looking glass she held in her palm. Seven wondrous days had passed since she and Tom and Billy recorded their claim at Solomon's Store; six days since she had purchased the looking glass.

Six days of hard digging and two pounds of gold—for each of them! If her brother Edward and her cousin Jonathan had come with her from Shawnee Mission, they would now be sharing in her claim. Her brothers had lived a harsh life too and deserved a few rewards. And she was sure her new friends, Tom and Billy, would've liked them tremendously.

With her shirt sleeve, Mary polished the looking glass. It had cost as much as a new shovel. But the cost did not matter; the mirror was a luxury she could now afford. She carefully stowed it on top of her Bible, her schoolbooks and her clothes inside the battered trunk at the foot of her bed.

After braiding her hair, she tucked her new corduroy pants into her boots and rolled up the sleeves of her red flannel shirt.

She patted her pouch and looped the silver chain of her new pocket watch through her belt. She then grabbed her trusty pack from a hook on the wall and made her way from the room.

Standing in the main room near the potbellied stove, Mary grabbed a still-warm biscuit her mother had left her. Though the cabin's windows didn't have glass panes, her inventive mother had used dozens of jars, just as she had in the bedrooms, to bring light into the main room. And her father had spent time and money to dig a foundation and lay plank floors—a rarity in mining towns, a fact Mary learned tromping through Midas' shops and the Queen of Sheba saloon.

"Soon I'll have enough to buy glass panes for our windows, Mother," Mary said out loud to herself. "And carpets for our floors, Father."

In contrast to the average miner's cabin, he had also invested the time to build the rough-hewn table and six chairs occupying the center of the main room. He'd built the bookcase that filled the wall between her bedroom and her parents', as well.

Three loud knocks on the door accompanied by Tom's and Billy's voices jolted Mary out of her daydream.

"Mary! You there?"

"C'mon out!"

Mary opened the door. A hundred feet beyond Tom and Billy, her parents were measuring a length of pine inside the wooden skeleton of the church.

"What's going on?" she asked, looking from one excited brother to the other.

"Solomon wants to meet with us!" Billy burst out. "In his fancy Intelligence Office – where he does all of his deep thinkin' and figurin', I suppose."

Tom nodded. "He wouldn't say what his plans were, but his eyes lit up and he smiled a lot and offered us cigars! Hope you don't mind, but Billy and I split yours."

Billy pulled out his two cigars for Mary and anyone else to see.

"Put those away!" Mary hissed quietly, shooting a glance at her parents. Luckily, their backs were turned. "My dad would kill me if he saw those cigars."

Tom cuffed his brother on the side of the head. "Wise up!"

Mary glared at Billy as he rubbed his sore ear.

"Let's get out of here," she urged, closing the door behind her, "before you get us all in a heap of trouble!"

CHAPTER 4

SOLOMON

SOLOMON Finch, founder of Midas, brushed the corners of his carefully clipped, black mustache with a long, unlit green cigar. His blue eyes gleamed, his closed mouth curling upward into a half smile.

He stood and brushed the front of his pinstriped dark gray vest. Solomon's perfectly white shirt collar was heavily starched, standing straight and touching his cleanly shaven cheeks.

But what caught Mary's attention was his tie pin. The pin was anything but typical. A nugget of solid gold, bigger than her thumb, held his red and green silk tie neatly in place.

"So glad you agreed to come!" Solomon said, sitting back down in the chair by his desk. He gestured toward a gold brocade couch. "Have a seat."

Mary and the brothers obeyed in unison. Mary had never seen the inside of the Intelligence Office before. The walls and ceilings were covered with handsome blue calico cloth, unlike the bleached cloth walls of Solomon's adjacent store. His mahogany desk, bookshelves and file cabinets looked recently oiled. The room had been swept of the dust and clumps of dried mud that plagued every dirt-floored building in Midas.

"I'm sure you're wondering why I asked you to come by," Solomon offered, running his cigar lengthwise beneath his nose before returning it to his vest pocket.

All three of them nodded at the same time.

Solomon smiled broadly. Mary held back a gasp—his front left tooth was made of polished gold!

"Frank, come here!" Solomon barked suddenly through the open door connecting the Intelligence Office and the store.

Moments later, Frank appeared. Mary recognized him immediately. He was the man who weighed their gold each day and had recorded their claim a week ago. Frank, like Solomon, wore pleated pants, a starched shirt and a pinstriped vest.

"Close the door and hustle that small table from the corner over here," Solomon commanded briskly while swiveling in his chair. He pulled a small map from the bookcase on his left. Frank set the table in front of Mary, who sat between the two brothers. Solomon unfolded the map and spread it over the table.

"Do you recognize what you're looking at?" Solomon asked, sounding cheerful again.

Mary and both brothers leaned forward and peered at the map. They all looked up with knowing expressions, but Mary spoke first.

"It's our claim and the Maidu's lake."

Solomon laughed and slapped his knees. "You're almost right! Past tense—was the Indians' lake. Now it's mine. Signed a contract yesterday with their leaders."

Mary's eyebrows rose sharply. "They sold it to you?"

"Sure did. Tough bargain, too. Cost me an arm and a leg." Solomon shook his head. "For the moment, I'd say them Indians got the better of the deal. Only time will tell."

Mary leaned forward to study the map again. "But why buy a lake?"

"Now that's a good question," Solomon chuckled, "wouldn't you say, Frank?"

"Yep," Frank answered with a grin.

"OK," Solomon continued, "have you ever heard about the Lake of Gold?"

Mary and the two brothers exchanged glances, then shook their heads.

"I didn't think so," Solomon said, playing with the ends of his moustache. "Frank used to work down south near Sutter's Fort, near the mill where Marshall discovered gold back in January of '48. Being the careful listener that Frank is, he heard many rumors."

Solomon leaned forward, his eyes narrowing.

"Like the Spaniards with their legend of El Dorado, the Indians have their legend too. The Yalesumni tribe believed in a Lake of Gold, somewhere near the headwaters of the Feather River. A lake high in the mountains, a lake that can't be seen from the river or the foothills—only from the highest peaks. Supposedly, the tribes who lived on the lake made fishhooks and arrowheads from the nuggets of gold that washed up at the water's edge."

Solomon paused to look Billy, then Tom, and finally Mary, straight in the eyes.

"That's why we bought the lake. You three may have discovered the entrance to the Lake of Gold."

Speechless, Mary and the brothers sank back into the couch.

"Here's the deal." Solomon turned and retrieved a sheet of paper from his desk. "We have a lake; you have the ravine where the lake drains into the North Fork. We don't need to discuss why that's important, except to say we need that ravine."

Solomon slapped the contract down on top of the map.

"Sign over your claim and I'll give each of you a one percent share in the Lake of Gold. You can continue to work the claim until Frank's crew needs access to the ravine. As partners in our new association, you can dig or mine anywhere that Frank's crews aren't working. Just don't get in their way or cause any trouble. Of course, any gold you find goes into the profit pool to be divvied up."

He pulled his cigar from his vest pocket and ran it beneath his nose. "If the three of you agree, we and our families will live in—well, to be blunt—excessive luxury for the rest of our lives. But all three of you must sign, or we don't have a deal."

Solomon leaned suddenly forward and perched on the edge of his seat. He broke into a wide smile, his gold tooth gleaming. A pen magically appeared in his hand.

CHAPTER 5

LIES

"No, Father!" Mary exclaimed, grabbing her father's calloused hands.

"Please! Standing up to Solomon won't change anything. He's already building the dam! Three crews work dawn to dusk. And he's posted sentries to keep the miners from Tent Town away. If you don't belong to the association, you might be shot!"

She stared into her father's stormy eyes. Anger clouded his brow. He squeezed her hands.

"Solomon cheated the Maidu. Someone must stand up to him."

Mary watched her father pull his hands away. Behind him, the afternoon sun bathed the skeletal church building. The church looked no more complete than it had three weeks earlier, the same day she and Tom and Billy met with Solomon and signed away their claim.

"You seem to know a great deal about the mining operation," her father said while staring downward toward Midas.

"Yes, I do." Mary played with the end of her long braid.

Silently her father nodded, his face still set toward Midas. "You're part of Solomon's association, aren't you?"

Mary bit her lip as a rosy bloom spread across her cheeks. "Yes, I own shares. So does Tom. And Billy."

Her father turned stiffly to face her. "How long have you

owned shares?"

"Three . . . weeks," Mary whispered.

Several seconds passed before he spoke, his voice thick with emotion.

"You've not only lied to your mother and me, you've betrayed the Maidu. Had you told me about this three weeks ago, I might have been able to do something. But not now."

Lines of pain crowded her father's eyes. "The renegades who signed the contract with Solomon are not even Maidu. The story is spreading. Everyone thinks it's a grand joke—red men trading their lake for two horses, a barrel of whiskey and new boots."

Mary pulled a loose strand of hair away from her face. She looked aside and waited, tight-lipped. The silence between her and her father deepened.

What could she say or do to prevent change from coming to the Sierras? What could Father do? Or the Maidu?

She had seen so much change in the two months since they had arrived from Shawnee Mission. Midas now covered the entire hillside. Instead of one hotel, there were three. Not one saloon, but four! And the number of flapping canvas lean-tos and tents in Tent Town never dropped below a hundred. Even mail came and went on a regular basis. So what if mailing a letter to Chicago, New York or Philadelphia cost $2.50. Drinking, gambling, cussing—men liked their freedom here. They did and said what they pleased. Took a bath when, or if, they wanted to. Spent a week's worth of sifting sand and gravel in a pan or rocker for a single night's sleep in a hotel and a hot meal. Or paid $12 for a jar of pickles. Didn't matter—money flowed like the water streaming out of the hills.

Sure, Mary knew what the Bible taught.

But here amid the snakes, the rocks, and the dust, the Bible didn't seem to work. Like her father's roofless church and its still pitifully small congregation. Besides her own family, only one other family—a young man and his pregnant wife who recently arrived from Pennsylvania—came Sunday mornings to sit on blanket-covered logs to sing hymns and to hear God's Word.

The touch of her father's hand on her forearm startled her.

"Mary," he said gravely, "as I shoed a Californio's horse in Midas this morning, men were talking about the Lake of Gold. I, too, have heard the legend about fishing hooks made from gold and about a nugget so large it could not be lassoed from the lake. I also heard that because Solomon has Californios working in his crews, he did not tell them the rest of that legend."

Mary looked up at last.

"The Yalesumni also believed that a demon spirit lived in the bottom of the lake. I do not believe in the legend about the lake, but I do believe a demon spirit inhabits these parts."

A demon? For a moment, Mary felt as if a dozen spiders crawled down her bare forearms. Her father continued.

"That demon's been around a long time, since before the days of our Lord Jesus himself. Today, men like Solomon worship this demon. The Spaniards, the English, the Romans, the Greeks—they all worshipped him too. Men have loved him from the beginning.

"The demon's name is Mammon. And no one has ever been able to serve both God and Mammon. Either he will hate the one and love the other, or hold to one and despise the other."

Her father pointed one hand toward Midas below, raising the other toward the church above.

His gentle eyes met hers. He spoke tenderly, but with conviction.

"Mary, you must choose this day whom you will serve. But as for our house, we will serve the Lord."

CHAPTER 6

LAKE OF GOLD

GOLDEN morning light filtered through the roof of Mary's lean-to.

With a long sigh, she returned her looking glass to its place atop her Bible and schoolbooks. She rolled up her blankets and gently stuffed them into the trunk. The fewer ants, the better, crawling about in her bedding come nighttime!

She stepped out of the lean-to. Her new home sat beneath an overhang of red rock beside a thicket of prickly brush.

Mary rolled up her shirtsleeves. She stepped toward the fire and the ring of flat stones she now used for her stovetop. She took a seat on a wide stump and moved her pan of cooling oats and honey to the wooden crate she used for a table. Next to the pan sat a tin cup full of freshly picked red gooseberries.

As Mary munched the berries, her gaze wandered over the old chokecherry and dogwood trees dotting the slopes, coming to rest on the oval, turquoise lake. She couldn't imagine how the lake—over a half-mile long and nearly three hundred yards wide—would look if Solomon succeeded in draining it dry.

Two miles away, out of sight and beyond the boulder-encrusted foothills across the lake, lay Midas. A little to the right, Mary envisioned the church and her home on the crest of the hill.

Mary lowered her head and stared at the fire. Each time she'd entered Midas during the last two weeks, she'd looked up the rocky path. Each time, she saw the church's wooden frame and a deep blue sky. And twice, when leaving Midas at evening, she found her father's lamp burning faintly at the top of the hill.

She could still hear his final words as clearly as when he had spoken them two weeks ago. Mary could still see the tear-streaked face of her mother as she stood trembling in the cabin doorway, begging her to stay.

Mary felt her cheeks grow hot. Stay or leave? Her father hadn't given her a real choice! Solomon offered her a chance for a better life now; her father offered her a life of sacrifice with the better life in the "hereafter."

Two sharp whistles echoed across the lake. Mary glanced up.

Both Tom and Billy waved from the rocky shoreline fifty feet below. After sharing her berries with them, she rinsed the pan in a pail of water and doused the fire.

Grabbing her pack, she headed toward the south end of the lake. For twenty minutes, they scurried over boulders and through clumps of brush. The lake narrowed into a rugged formation of steep slopes, heavy brush, scraggly red firs and a 15-foot waterfall.

Climbing up through the firs, they entered a shadowy crevice in the hillside. They walked beside the stream that fed the waterfall, and emerged from the crevice on a wide bed of smooth stones.

They were greeted by bright sunlight, a thick stand of red pines and a towering wooden dam spanning a wide ravine.

The unfinished dam stood nearly thirty feet tall and sixty feet wide. Fifty men labored under the barking commands of four crew leaders. Frank and his German engineer, Hans, supervised from behind a table of rough-hewn planks. Hans wore short, leather pants, a white shirt and a Panama hat. He shuffled the large drawings he used to guide the construction. The crews called Frank "General" and Hans "Colonel," even though neither had ever been officers.

Several of the lake's smaller feeder streams had been diverted from the lake via flumes—wooden chutes that carried stream or river water above the ground. But here, at the lake's largest stream, a dam was required. Hans had cautioned Solomon about starting the dam with autumn but one month away. With autumn came rain, and rain was a miner's most dreaded enemy.

Mary surveyed the site. Hans had built the dam from the outside edges of the ravine in toward the middle, leaving a narrow channel for the rushing stream to squeeze its way through—like Billy squirting water through the gap between his two front teeth!

Frank waved a red bandana above his head. Within seconds, the four crew leaders signaled their teams. Saws, sledgehammers and pickaxes clanked to a standstill.

"Today's the day!" Billy said to Mary. "We're lucky to see it!"

Suspended by a long chain, a rough-cut log ten feet long and thick as a big man's waist hung from a winch above the narrow channel. Creaking, the winch lowered the log into the rushing water. The stream bounded easily over the log and slammed it into place against the sidewalls of the dam. By the third log, huge fans of white water twice the height of a man splashed into the air over the growing wall. By the fifth, water lapped in wide, lazy tongues over the top of the logs. By the seventh, the increased pressure forced hissing sprays of water through spaces between the logs, dousing everyone with a man-made rainstorm.

"Yahoo!" Frank yelled, waving his bandana and leading a chorus of shouts and cheers. A flock of hats were launched high into the air. Arms and hands waved wildly.

Now, while half the crews finished shoring up the dam, Frank would send the remaining crews to where she and Tom and Billy had first made their claim. There, the crews would begin cutting deep channels in the ravine—and empty the lake's trapped waters into the North Fork.

Mary knelt beside the trickling remains of the once-powerful stream. Her eyes widened as she sucked in a deep breath.

Sunlight glittered off long threads of golden flakes woven through the sand and gravel.

Mary stood, her heart pounding. She spun around, letting her gaze follow the streambed into the shadowy crevice leading to the waterfall and the lake.

If the glittering streambed gave any indication of what lay beneath the placid waters of the lake, then they had indeed discovered the fabled Lake of Gold!

CHAPTER 7

QUEEN OF SHEBA

As evening settled in, Mary paused in the rutted street outside the Queen of Sheba saloon. Tom and Billy pushed through the swinging wooden doors and bounded inside ahead of her. She turned and stared up at the foothills rising to the east.

A shimmering yellow light caught her eye—her father's lantern. Fighting back a tug of homesickness, she straightened her shoulders. Mary knew word had spread that she'd left home to live by the lake. Every day her father labored at the foundry, she knew he endured the disgrace of her leaving home.

Mary passed through the swinging doors. She stood just inside a brightly lit room with walls of red cloth. To either side, miners, both young and old, jostled for places around poker tables and gaming wheels. Directly ahead stretched a plank-topped bar, packed shoulder-to-shoulder with boisterous, thirsty miners. Fog-like smoke wafted through the saloon. Glasses clinked and tin cups clanged. Spilled drinks made puddles on the dirt floor.

She looked to the back corner of the room. Tom waved from the stairs leading to the second floor.

She avoided the puddles and the rowdy miners.

"Hurry!" Tom said. "The meetin's about to start!"

Boots clopping, Mary quickly climbed the stairs and took a seat beside Tom on a bench in the back of the room.

The hubbub of voices and angry faces surprised Mary. Normally, the Lake of Gold weekly shareholder meeting began peacefully.

"Enough!" Solomon bellowed, standing at the front of the room. He held out his hands to quiet the crowd. "Take your seats, or I'll cancel this meeting!"

The grumbling slowly died down as men took their seats. Some shook fists. Some cussed.

Mary lowered her head and tried to block out the shameful language. She wondered what her father would say if he saw her among these crude men. The thought made her neck burn with embarrassment.

When she finally looked up, she noticed a black-headed ranchero at the front of the room standing to Solomon's right. His broad shoulders and straight stance, his oiled hair, his deeply tanned and weathered face, his dark eyes and trimmed mustache gave him a commanding presence—not to mention his short leather jacket, velvet trousers, red silk waistcoat and embroidered shirt.

Mary had heard about the rancheros, wealthy Californios who had stayed after the treaty with Mexico, when California became a U.S. territory. Some rancheros owned hundreds of thousands of acres and raised vast herds of cattle and sheep.

Solomon turned from the crowd and faced the ranchero. "If what you say is true, Ignácio del Valles, surely you will urge your fellow Californios to continue working on the dam. If they leave now, our venture will suffer. If our venture suffers, Midas will suffer. Your sister and her husband's hotel will suffer too."

The ranchero's eyes twinkled. And though the situation seemed serious, Mary thought she saw a smile beginning to form.

Straightening his shoulders, he tugged at his vest, then spoke. "I doubt I have such power. However, if you offer shares, even small shares, to my fellow Californios, I believe they will continue to serve you and build the dam."

Solomon thrust out his hands to keep the other shareholders' voices from erupting again.

"After all," Señor Valles added, tilting his head as his eyes searched the room, "they have heard that even a young woman can own shares in the Lake of Gold."

Suddenly, Mary found herself staring into the ranchero's eyes. A hint of amusement lingered on his face. Alarmed by his attention, she looked quickly away.

Chair legs scraped on the floorboards. Every head turned. Suddenly she found herself the focus of a room full of men.

Mortified, Mary stood up and started for the door. Tom and Billy jumped to their feet. She ran down the steps. Hurrying past the bar, she pushed her way between two full-bearded miners who smelled like the whiskey sloshing in their glasses. In seconds, she burst through the swinging doors, stopping in the street. The late evening air felt instantly cool on her cheeks.

"Ooh, ooh!" Mary huffed loudly, balling her hands into fists. She wanted to slug the Californio for saying what he did! She and Tom and Billy had traded their claim for shares—fair and square! Those Californios Solomon had hired were only laborers.

There was a thud of boots behind her. She spun around, expecting to see Tom and Billy.

To her surprise, she found herself facing the sharply dressed ranchero who had singled her out. He carried her pack over one arm. Only then did Mary realize that she'd left it inside.

"Señorita, you must accept my apologies," Ignácio said with a short bow, holding out her pack. "I asked your two friends to allow me the chance to make amends."

His eyes and face beamed both honest intent and humility.

Mary glanced up. Tom and Billy waved from between the parted saloon doors, then disappeared back inside.

She reached out and warily grabbed her pack.

Before she could thank him, the ranchero continued.

"I did not seek to humiliate you, but to perhaps persuade Señor Solomon to treat my countrymen more fairly. I know what he pays the other miners in his crew. You have heard of a 'digger's ounce,' have you not?"

Mary looked down. She'd heard the townspeople and the miners joke about it. When a Maidu paid gold for goods, a shop owner or trader would use a two-ounce weight instead of a regular one-ounce weight. So, when a Maidu paid in gold, he paid twice what a man with white, black or even yellow skin would pay. And apart from cheating them, the name 'digger,' as the Maidu were often called, was offensive to them.

"Please let me show my sincerity," the ranchero continued. "My sister and her family own a hotel here in Midas—La Casa Amparo. Be our guest for a hot meal, por favor.

"Your father has always done such excellent work shoeing my horses. And he treats my sister and her husband with respect. I would consider your presence an honor, and a way to express my thanks to him."

A smile warmed his face.

"So, you will accept?"

Mary returned his smile.

CHAPTER 8
IGNÁCIO

MARY savored the corn soup, the fire-grilled beef, the plump cilantro-sprinkled tomatoes, and the freshly baked bread. When had she tasted such good food? Four months ago, back in Kansas? Most miners could not afford such a feast.

Ignácio's sister, Carolina, refilled the breadbasket. She wore a dotted silk dress and silk stockings, and a short sleeveless jacket. Brightly colored ribbons were woven through her long black hair.

Her husband, Julio, tucked his felt hat, decorated with silver braids, under his arm. He smiled broadly at Ignácio and Mary, then bowed his head. "Adios, Señor—Señorita. Good night."

Her eight-year-old twins, Isabel and Ramón, grinned and waved. Julio gently placed his hands on their shoulders and ushered them from the room.

"Please excuse my husband. His day never ends," Carolina explained. "At daybreak, he rises and feeds the pigs. At night, he tends to the needs of our guests."

Night! Mary gripped the arms of her chair. She glanced out the window to the street. The evening had vanished into darkness.

Ignácio noted the alarm skittering across her face. "Do not worry. My sister would be delighted to have you as a guest tonight at La Casa Amparo."

Mary started to protest. A room in a hotel like this could run

$50 a night! But Ignácio held up his hand, his eyes twinkling just as they had in the meeting room when he first stood up to Solomon.

His sister laughed. "Please accept our offer, or he will be grumpy for the rest of his visit!"

Mary grinned and looked down at her plate.

"I will take that as a yes," Ignácio said happily. "Now, I want to tell you a rumor I have heard—and I have heard many rumors these past two days. One I found most interesting: that a young lady has chosen to make the Lake of Gold, as Señor Solomon refers to it, her home—while it is yet a lake."

Snorting, Carolina sawed angrily at her beefsteak.

"Please forgive my sister's dislike for Señor Solomon," Ignácio said with a wry smile. He leaned back in his chair. "So now, I ask that young lady of the rumor: Why do you live by the lake?"

Mary breathed deeply, then lifted her eyes. "If you know my father, then you know about his work among the Maidu."

Listening intently, Ignácio nodded.

"We have always been a missionary family. Always. Moving from state to state. We've even been as far north as Ontario, Canada! He teaches them how to survive the loss of their lands. Teaches them new trades, new skills. Teaches them the Bible."

Ignácio tilted his head slightly. "And he also teaches them how to forgive, does he not? Your father is a wise man. We Californios understand the plight of the Maidu far too well. I fear we will soon be treated like them, cheated of what is ours and driven off our lands and claims.

"I am a blessed man," the ranchero said, placing his hands on his chest. "But many Californios are not so blessed. And so, just like the others, they have caught what my ancestors called 'la fiebre del oro.'"

"La fe-ay-bray del oro?" Mary repeated, leaning forward.

"Gold fever," Ignácio said. His eyes drooped and lost their

sparkle. "The fever is like a wild plague, striking young and old. Soldiers desert their posts. Teachers close their schools. In San Francisco, hundreds of ships now rot in the harbor, and no one cares about the cargo. Even San Francisco's newspaper closed its doors.

"Just a year ago, everyone lived in harmony. White men, black men, Californios, Chinese and, sometimes, even Indians worked side by side. In '48, placer gold, the gold easily mined by pickaxe or pan, was plentiful. In those days a miner could leave sacks of gold dust in plain sight and no one would steal it! Today, placer gold is not so easily found. Miners forage the land and rivers like plagues of locusts. They dig longer, harder, but find less gold! The goodwill between men of different colors has been replaced with envy and distrust. And those of us who have lived here all our lives are no longer welcome. Such irony! We, the Californios, taught the Easterners how to pan their gold!"

Ignácio paused, drumming his fingers on the chair arm. "You must understand something. 'La fiebre del oro' is not new to the Americas. Three hundred years ago, my Spanish ancestors came searching for El Dorado. They, like miners today, were possessed by the fever. My ancestors took no care for those they conquered. They brought diseases that would kill more terribly than war. They came for El Dorado. Do you know what the name means?"

Mary shook her head.

"It means 'the gilded one.' The legend of El Dorado is known throughout South America: a city built completely of gold and hidden in the middle of the jungle. But El Dorado was also the name of the city's king because, as the legend goes, he gilded or covered himself with gold dust.

"Later, however, the South Americans told the story of El Dorado to Spanish explorers to hurry them away from Indian cities and homelands. As you might know, the Spaniards spent years trying to find the city. Every time they sought directions from those early Americans, the explorers were told, 'Nah, too far south. Keep going. Can't be far now. Just ahead.'"

Carolina chuckled and dabbed her mouth with a napkin.

Mary laughed. "Then it's only a legend!"

"Perhaps," he replied, his eyes twinkling again. "But California is rich with gold. And la fiebre del oro is as real as the gold, as you yourself can attest."

The humor of the moment faded abruptly. Mary sat up straight.

Ignácio softened his voice. "Do not be offended by what I say. Most men do not realize that it is God who gives the power to make wealth. And most, once they find wealth, do not thank God for his generous kindness.

"Instead of worshiping God, they worship what he gives them. And to them, what God gives is never enough. Coveting is easy. Being content is hard—at times, beyond what one can bear."

Ignácio folded his napkin and laid it beside his plate.

"God has seen the sacrifices your family has made for others. In his time, I believe with all of my heart that he will reward you. Perhaps in ways you can not now imagine.

"But this truth I share with you," he said, the twinkle in his eyes vanishing suddenly. Both his gaze and his voice hardened.

"Gold is friend to no man. Do not trust it! For what does it profit you, to gain the whole world, but lose your own soul?"

CHAPTER 9

THE CAVE

MARY returned from her morning trek along the lake and dropped her pack by the lean-to. Her stomach growling noisily, she rummaged through her tent for the crackers and the beef jerky she planned for her midday meal.

Five weeks had passed since her night at La Casa Amparo. But she could still smell the sizzling beef, still feel the luxurious softness of the feather bed. And she could still remember looking out the hotel window and seeing her father's lantern burning high and bright upon the hill.

She hadn't felt this excited since the day she'd first discovered gold and they'd recorded their claim. As she munched on a cracker, she raised a hand to shield her eyes from the bright sun. Where were Tom and Billy?

Autumn had arrived, but the lake still shimmered with purples and blues and greens. Solomon had ignored Ignácio's advice, and the Californios had left. But Frank's remaining crews didn't lag behind. Boosted by a pledge of higher wages, the crews increased their pace and completed the dam ahead of schedule. At the same time, new crews hefted pickaxes and shovels to the ravine where she and the brothers had first staked their claim. The clatter of metal against rock rang day after day as they dug the channel that would drain the lake. Or in Frank's own words, "pull the plug," as if the lake was nothing but a huge bathtub.

But then they'd struck bedrock and were forced to dig shallow. So, when the channel finally reached the lake, the outflow of water was only a third of what Hans had hoped for. In spite of the dam blocking water at one end and the channel draining water out at the other end, the level of the lake had dropped only two feet. Meanwhile, the dam was creating a second lake from the swelling backwaters.

Stumped, Frank and Hans could come up with only one idea— dig a second channel. So, the clatter of pickaxe and shovel on rock resumed, faster and louder.

Each morning Solomon rode horseback to the diggings. Each passing day he shouted louder, demanding that Frank and Hans find a quicker solution. Who knew when the rains might begin? Each evening he rode off "spitting mad," as Billy liked to say.

Shortly after the sun cleared the hillside, Mary heard the brothers' familiar whistling echo across the lake. She tossed her clean pans into her lean-to.

"Hey, guys!" Mary yelled, standing and waving.

Mary dropped the flap to her lean-to as the brothers entered her campsite.

Tom propped a leg on the stump she used for a chair. "So sorry that my folks refused to take you in. But they didn't want to get on your papa's bad side."

Mary smiled weakly. "I didn't want to get on his bad side, either."

"Well, back to business. Billy and I think the crews have abandoned the second channel. Looks like now they're diggin' themselves a couple of coyote holes."

Billy nodded and tossed a small stone into the fire. A puff of sparks and ash rose and whirled into the air.

"Coyote holes?" Mary folded her arms. Most miners feared coyote holes—narrow tunnels burrowed horizontally into a hillside. Lucky miners wriggled into the deep tunnels and found underground gold beds trapped in ancient river channels. Others clawed for daylight when the tunnels collapsed on top of them. Some poor souls had woken to meet their Maker.

Mary swallowed hard. God forbid that from ever happening to her!

"Wanna go and see?" Billy asked.

"I've found something more exciting than a coyote hole!" Mary said, shaking her head and grabbing her pack. "Come on!"

She led Tom and Billy along the shore toward the dam, refusing to divulge her secret.

Twenty minutes later, Mary paused at the foot of what had once been a fifteen-foot waterfall. Now, only four inches of clear, flowing water splashed down over the tall stone steps—seepage from the dam.

"You call this exciting?" Tom asked, thumbing the brim of his hat.

"You just can't see it yet." Mary turned and climbed the rocky hillside just to the left of the stone steps.

She grabbed the exposed roots of an old tree to pull herself up to a small ledge overgrown by thorny brush.

"Can you see it now?" She smiled smugly and sat on the ledge, avoiding the small green thorns. She wound her long braid on top of her head and stuffed it beneath her old leather cap.

Billy thumped his brother on the shoulder. "Yeah, yeah! Mary found a cave!"

Tom took two steps forward, peering past Mary into the dark and nearly invisible opening. Before the dam, when the waterfall ran free and wild, the opening had been hidden and unreachable.

Mary stood up. "Well, what are you two waiting for?"

CHAPTER 10

DISCOVERY

Mary turned sideways, ducked her head and entered the cave. Her cap brushed the root-covered ceiling. A cascade of fine dirt and tiny bits of stone bounced off her cap and down the front of her shirt.

Once she was through the narrow opening, Tom handed her the pack. She moved farther inside. Moments later, Tom and Billy stood inside the bright opening, brushing dirt from their shirts.

Mary knelt. She opened her pack and removed a lantern.

"Where do you think this leads?" Tom asked.

"Don't know," she answered. After two strikes, the wick burst into flame. The darkness fled, revealing a narrow stone corridor.

"Ready?" she asked, turning up the lantern.

The brothers nodded. Mary led the way, holding the lantern out in front of her. The rocky floor sloped downward to the right. Immediately, Mary felt the temperature drop several degrees.

"Caves get pretty cool," Mary explained. "But once you're down a little ways, the temperature stops falling."

Several minutes later, Mary paused. The floor angled sharply down before leveling into a wide chamber. She worked her way to the bottom, her boots scraping down the rough surface. Tom and Billy followed quickly, bounding down and spraying dirt against Mary's boots as they skidded to a halt behind her.

Mary raised the lantern again and moved forward. Ahead, the sphere of light revealed an opening. As they drew nearer, she observed the opening was shaped like a T, leading left and right.

"Which way?" she asked, glancing back. The lantern cast their shadows onto the chamber floor behind them.

Tom stepped up to look over Mary's shoulder, then suddenly slapped the back of his neck. "Hey! Somethin's crawling on me!" he said, quickly running his hand under his collar.

"What is it?" Billy said, ducking slightly.

"I really don't wanna' know!" Mary chimed in. Goose bumps prickled down her shoulders and arms.

"Yuck!" Tom wiped a spider's gooey remains on his pants leg.

Mary lightly bit her lip. Lantern light revealed dozens of gossamer strands filling the T.

"Guys, look around. I need something to clear these webs."

She raised the lantern. The rectangular chamber where they stood cleared the tops of their hats by several inches. Water trickled among the smooth rocks, large and small, littering the chamber.

Tom's legs disappeared into the shadows as he stepped behind a boulder. Something other than boot leather scraped noisily across the rock floor, then snapped, like a small stick breaking.

Tom stooped over. "Hey, here's something that might work!"

For a second, Mary could make out only the peak of Tom's hat in the lantern light. Then he stood up, smiling at his find.

But instead of a stick, Tom clutched a long, white bone in one hand. Mary shrieked. The brothers laughed.

"Belonged to a deer, I'd say." Still chuckling, Tom stepped from behind the boulder. He turned the bone over in his hand.

Billy agreed. "Yeah, but look at those scrape marks. Somethin' gnawed it clean!"

Mary shifted her eyes from the gnawed bone. Billy's and Tom's smiling faces suddenly darkened with worry.

"You thinking what I'm thinking?" Mary asked, swallowing hard.

Tom started to reply when a deep growl echoed across the cave.

The two brothers froze like statues, except for two pairs of wide-open eyes that moved to lock onto Mary's.

Twenty feet away, at the foot of the incline, the largest bear Mary had ever seen rose on its hind legs. Lifting its massive brown head, the bear growled a second time through its gaping pink maw.

Mary spun and ran, the brothers scrambling behind her.

She turned left at the T, leading with the lantern and pushing her hand, arm and face through the layers of spider webs draped across the corridor. The passageway twisted sharply to the right. She squinted and pressed her lips together tightly as the thin webs clung to her cheeks and nose and eyelashes.

Then suddenly, as she clawed the webs from her face, Mary found herself at the rocky edge of a swiftly moving underground stream. Over ten feet wide, it was too far to jump across!

The two brothers skidded behind her, knocking Mary forward.

With a scream, she stumbled feet first into the stream. Splashing, she thrust the lantern above her head. To her surprise, the bitterly cold water was only waist deep. And though the stream forced her slowly forward, she was able to keep her balance.

A roar echoed behind Tom and Billy. Mary fought against the push of the stream and glanced over her shoulder.

"Jump!" she yelled. "Jump!"

The brothers hesitated, but a third and louder roar sent them leaping into the air. With twin splashes, they landed in the stream.

The bear padded to the watery ledge, roaring and swiping at the air with a huge paw, waving its unwelcome visitors away.

The water shoved Mary firmly in the back, propelling her around a dark corner between narrowing stone walls. Bubbling fiercely around her, the water rose from her waist to her chin.

Mary gasped as the water lapped up around the base of the lantern. If the light went out . . .

But as quickly as the water rose, it fell as the walls of the cave widened right and left. The stream, now only knee-deep, slowed enough for Mary to work her way to a gravelly shore.

"Thank you, dear God," she uttered. Shivering violently, she stepped out of the stream onto a stone shelf. With every upward step, the lantern's yellow glow pushed back more darkness.

Tom and Billy dragged themselves from the stream behind her, teeth chattering, water sluicing out of their clothes.

"I'm freezing!" Billy said, squeezing water from his shirt.

"At least you're not bear food!" Tom chided, brushing his hair back from his face with both hands.

"Guys, forget about . . . the bear."

The brothers looked up, their mouths falling open.

Yellow light reflected off the cave wall back onto Mary's pale face and trembling blue lips. Water dripped from her chin as her disbelieving eyes slowly moved from left to right.

A gleaming band of gold, nearly twenty feet long and varying in thickness from one to three feet, angled down through a wall of yellow and white quartz.

Mary's eyes narrowed, then blinked. She inched forward.

Carved directly into the gold were the artistic glyphs of an unknown native scribe. A mural of men with drawn bows. Horses. Cone-shapes she recongized as teepees. Mothers with papooses. A lake surrounded by mountains.

Stepping back a little, she studied the glyphs on the angling band of gold. Though she couldn't figure out what all of the markings meant, the scribe had grouped the markings in obvious sections, starting left and working right.

"We're gonna be rich!" Billy chirped.

"Filthy rich—if we can find our way out of here," Tom added, licking his lips, his eyes riveted on the gold.

Mary listened to the brothers as they one-upped each other on how they would spend their fortunes.

La fiebre del oro. Ignácio's words whispered through her thoughts.

Gold fever, as real as the gold itself.

Mary shuddered, whether from her wet clothes or from Ignácio's words, she wasn't sure. La fiebre del oro would soon destroy the history of the tribe recorded on this gold and crystalline wall.

"Hey look!" Billy called. The stream narrowed and continued down a tunnel leaving the chamber. "I think I mighta found a way outta here!"

CHAPTER 11

INQUISITION

SOLOMON'S unlit cigar that had been wedged between his fingers dropped to the floor. He turned disbelieving eyes toward Mary and the two brothers perched on the couch.

"Twenty feet of gold?" Solomon questioned in a gruff voice. "If this is a prank, you'll pay for it!"

Frank sat in a wooden chair beside the closed door of the Intelligence Office.

"They're telling the truth," he said. "Me and Hans found them squeezing out that crevice in front of the dam. They were excited and soaked to the bone. And their story hasn't changed one iota."

Tom nodded and swallowed hard. "We all saw it, sir!"

"A vein of gold running through a wall of crystal!" Solomon's voice cracked with excitement.

"Probably quartz," Frank said, rubbing his chin.

Solomon picked up his cigar from the floor and dusted it off.

Mary lowered her gaze and folded her hands. Any hope of saving the beautiful glyphs and the history they told was now gone.

"And access to the cave?" Solomon asked.

Tom looked at Billy, then to Solomon and Frank. "Only from the entrance at the waterfall. Getting to the cave through the underground river tunnel would be impossible."

Frank nodded. "Hans already tried, but he couldn't get more than halfway into the crevice. And he's not a big man."

Solomon bit off the end of his cigar, spitting the loose piece of tobacco into a tall brass spittoon beside his desk.

"Doesn't matter. That cave's not going anywhere tonight. We'll check it out ourselves tomorrow morning, bear or no bear. The fact that we never found those caves ourselves upsets me greatly."

Frank protested weakly, but Solomon ignored him. He lit his cigar, puffed hard three times, then blew a lazy smoke ring out of his mouth. He reached over to his desk and scooped up a handful of cigars from his humidor.

"Here you go, boys," he said, offering them to Tom and Billy.

Billy grimaced. "No thanks. Those last ones turned me green."

Tom shook his head. "Same here."

Solomon smiled, his gold tooth shining. "Well, well. Your loss is my gain."

He glanced to Frank, then back to the brothers and Mary.

"I guess that concludes this meeting. Right, Frank?"

"Right, Boss."

"You three are free to go. For such a fine job, stop by the Queen of Sheba. Dinner's on me. Anything you want."

Frank opened the door. Tom led the way out, with Mary following. Just before the door closed behind her, she spied Solomon winking at Frank.

On a hunch, Mary grabbed Tom's and Billy's arms. She quickly surveyed the store. No customers were at the counter, and the clerk was busily stocking canned goods on a shelf across the room.

Mary whispered. "Just stand there a second and shield me. Don't say anything and just pretend that everything's normal."

Turning, she dropped to one knee. She brought her ear up to the keyhole. The voices were muffled, but she could still make out

Solomon's voice.

"The Lake of Gold!" Solomon exclaimed. "El Dorado at last!"

"Yeah, and to think how cheap you got it," Frank said with a short laugh. "Signing that contract with them renegades from Mexico—for liquor and supplies."

Solomon laughed too. "Some of those savages don't even wear clothes. What do they need gold for? Let 'em find somewhere else to live."

"The timing is so perfect," Frank added. "We just finished digging the coyote holes. The blasting powder arrived from San Francisco this afternoon. Tomorrow we'll start excavating the cave, blow the coyote holes and drain the lake—all in one day!"

"And now our profits will soar even higher since we fudged the account books. Those kids and the other shareholders will never know how much we lowered their take."

Solomon chortled, deep and long. Frank joined in.

Mary slowly rose to her feet, her eyes narrowing. How foolish the three of them had been—rooked out of their rightful rewards!

As she stepped between Tom and Billy toward the open door and the street, her shoulders sagged and her heart sank.

How foolish!

CHAPTER 12
EVIDENCE

SOLOMON's a big cheat," Tom complained. He mopped his biscuit in the greasy pork gravy, then stuffed it into his mouth.

"And a liar." Mary wrapped her hands around her mug of tea.

"So what can we do?" Billy asked, plopping chunks of raw onion into his bowl of black beans.

"Nothing, really. He's thought it all through," Mary mused. "Tomorrow, Solomon and Frank will figure out a way to dig the gold out of the crystal wall, and the picture history of the lake tribe will be lost forever. Then they'll blow their coyote holes and drain the lake. And on top of that, they're swindling us."

Tom and Billy grew silent, picking at their meals.

Mary stared into her mug and wondered about the vein of gold and the markings. Who had carved the glyphs into the gold? The Maidu? Or maybe some earlier tribe who lived at the time Ignácio's Spanish ancestors first searched for El Dorado.

"Somebody's got to stand up to him," Billy moaned.

"Who'd believe us?" Tom said, shaking his head. "Don't have any evidence, only what Mary heard through the door. It's her word against his. If Mary goes toe-to-toe with Solomon, guess who's gonna be left standing?"

Frowning, Mary set her mug down. Tom was right. Without some physical evidence that revealed the truth—Solomon wouldn't be budged. If only she had listened to her father!

Her eyes narrowed suddenly and she chewed lightly on her lip. Evidence? She quickly pieced together an idea.

Were Solomon's feet planted on rock, or shifting sand? Had he? Could they? What if?

Her eyes lighting up, she pounded her fists on the table.

"Guys! Maybe there is something we can do. Something that Solomon can't lie his way out of!"

Mary bolted to her feet and grabbed her pack.

"Wh-what're you going to do?" Billy asked, standing up.

"Not me—we. It'll take all three of us to make this work."

She parted the Queen of Sheba's swinging doors with a hard shove. A light breeze brushed across her face as she stepped into the street.

Her eyes were drawn up the hill east of town. Her father's lantern, like a tiny orb, glowed yellow against the black backdrop of the hill. But tonight, unlike other nights, there was a dark sky. Not a single star.

Mary heard the creak of the swinging doors behind her, followed by the thud of boots.

"OK, what next?" Tom asked from behind her, his voice shaky.

Mary glanced down the street to Solomon's Store and saw the glow of lamp light out the open front door.

Pulling her knife from its sheath, she dropped to one knee. She explained her idea and etched a diagram in the dirt. With the tip of the knife, she made more marks on the diagram, then went over the sequence of the events and when they needed to happen.

"So, do you think you can do it?" she asked with a sly grin.

Tom tapped his lip. "Sure, why not? You agree, Billy?"

Billy scrunched his face and nodded at the same time.

"I'll take that as a yes." Mary stood and sheathed her knife. "And don't worry—Ignácio's sister will agree. Trust me!"

Tom and Billy cut between two buildings and raced up the

steep hill to the upper section of the road—the shortest route to La Casa Amparo.

Mary headed toward Solomon's Store. She took a deep breath before entering.

She glanced around. Several miners and a Chinese laundry owner milled around looking at supplies. Directly opposite the front door, Frank stood behind a counter, chatting with two Negro miners. Frank was working alone!

Mary smiled, walked inside and turned left just as she had a dozen times before. She worked her way slowly along the front shelves, studying the goods. Pickles. Smoked halibut. Dried beef tongue. Butter crackers. Dried apples. China bread. Every two steps she paused to pick up a jar or box and pretended to read the label.

She barely listened to Frank and the miners trade stories and jokes. Instead, she fought back the jittering in her hands and knees.

Where were Tom and Billy?

She reached the end of the aisle. As she turned to face the second row of shelves behind her, she glanced left. The door to Solomon's Intelligence Office was unlatched! And the band of yellow light beneath the door meant a lantern burned inside.

Boots thumped heavily on the wood floor, followed by Tom's voice. "Hey, Frank!"

Rising on her toes, Mary peered through the shelves.

The Negro miners stepped to the side as Tom and Billy approached the counter. Billy clutched an old burlap sack with both hands—a grain sack that started making noises.

The miner's eyes popped open wide. "Boy's got 'im a pig!"

Billy grinned. "You wanna buy it? Look's good, don't it?"

Before Frank or the miners could answer, Billy knelt down and opened the sack. He reached inside.

The young, frightened and well-greased pig squealed, then squirmed from Billy's hands and shot out of the bag.

Startled, the miners jumped back. One of them knocked over a small display decorated with a bearded miner's smiling face and colorful lettering that read: Dr. Dill's Burnt Rhubarb Extract! Excellent For Diarrhea And Other Intestinal Infirmities. Small brown bottles bounced across the counter.

Frank scowled as he waved his hands. "Catch it!"

Tom's and Billy's maneuvers cornered the pig to the right side of the store, drawing everyone's attention.

Mary stepped quickly to her left and pushed open the door to the Intelligence Office. She slipped inside and closed the door closed behind her.

The hairs on her arm stood on end, but Mary hurried to Solomon's desk. She hastily shuffled through the papers on his desktop, then the drawers. Even though she'd closed the door, she could still hear loud voices and the squealing pig.

Seconds! She only had seconds! Where could it be?

To the left of his desk stood a bookcase. Many weeks ago, hadn't Solomon taken his map of the lake from one of its shelves?

Yes! The map. And beneath the map, a thin leather satchel.

Mary yanked the satchel open—the Lake of Gold account book! She yanked out the book, stuffed it into her pack, then replaced the satchel beneath the map.

Then she was at the door, cracking it ajar. The two miners were guffawing now, slapping their thighs. Frank knelt on the dirt floor and scooped up the dried beans and rice that had spilled when Tom struggled to put the pig back into the sack.

Seconds later, she stood behind Tom and Billy and the pig.

"You're all troublemakers!" Frank boomed. "You're gonna pay for this right out of your shares! Now get outta here!"

"Yes, sir!" Tom and Billy said in unison.

In the darkness between the buildings across the street, Mary showed Tom and Billy her find. They agreed to meet at daybreak. The brothers grinned as they strutted off to return the pig to

Carolina.

Five minutes later, Mary plunked down two of her four remaining ten-dollar pieces for a room—of sorts. She didn't dare try to find her way to the lake at night, as important as it was to get there soon. Clutching her pack tightly, she walked to the back of the stables and slowly climbed the ladder to the hayloft.

But sleep would not come, despite the comforting feel of the pack stowed against her side, the gentle patter of rain on the tin roof above her head, and the uncertain prayers that stumbled haltingly from her lips.

CHAPTER 13

TRAPPED

MARY and the two brothers hurried along the shore of the lake through rain and the gray morning light. A blanket of charcoal clouds crept steadily over the Sierras, blocking the rising sun.

Mary adjusted her oilskin poncho to deflect the water streaming from her cap. And though weary from a lack of sleep, she pressed on behind Tom and Billy to the end of the lake. At the foot of the waterfall, they found three large boulders fairly close together, took a seat in the rain, and waited for Solomon to arrive.

The sky had lightened, but the rain was still falling when the figures of Solomon, Frank, and Hans first appeared. The three dark, horse-mounted silhouettes came to a halt thirty feet away when the lead horse slowed.

All three men wore brown oilskins and wide-brimmed hats. Something in their posture worried Mary. Solomon and his men seemed unconcerned that his account book had been stolen, in fact, he was smiling.

But now it was too late to run.

"Well, well," Solomon said, dismounting. His deep, surly voice sounded tired, like he too had not slept. "Talk about luck, Frank. Never expected to find these three here."

Frank, the rider to the left, mumbled angrily.

"So . . ." Solomon sneered, "let's see if I've figured this one out.

After our meeting, you must've been eavesdropping at my office door. Heard me and Frank talking about the fixes to our account book. Then you boys played a little game with Frank. Used the pig to distract him. And you, young lady, snuck into my office and rifled my records. Stealing's a pretty serious crime."

Solomon splashed a half dozen steps forward. "But I give you this, you're clever. And because you're clever, I'm willing to deal. Return my record book and I won't press charges. No trial, no jail time, no trouble with parents for our little trio of thieves. Sound fair?"

As Solomon spoke, Hans and Frank dismounted from their horses. Frank stepped wide to one side, Hans to the other.

"Hold it right there," Mary said, standing up on her boulder.

Solomon raised a hand. Frank and Hans stopped advancing.

Mary blew a big drop of water from the tip of her nose. "Trio of thieves? Now I'd say that's the pot calling the kettle black!"

Solomon laughed hard, turning and winking first to Frank and then to Hans, while sloshing forward another two steps.

"I think I'm plumb out of patience with this whippersnapper of a girl," Solomon said with a smile that fell suddenly into a humorless, flat line.

"OK, boys, time to round 'em up," he said as he pulled a long-barreled pistol from beneath his coat.

No sooner had Solomon spoken, than a thunderous boom echoed across the lake. The ground shook. Mary lost her balance. She jumped from the boulder to the hillside near the waterfall. Tom and Billy lept down near her.

Despite the rain, Frank ripped off his hat. "They've started blasting the coyote holes! They were supposed to wait for us!"

"Forget the blasting! Grab them kids!" Solomon roared, waving his pistol.

Mary led the scramble up the hillside toward the cave. Struggling to keep her footing, she grabbed an old root by the mouth of the cave and pulled herself up.

Tom and Billy were not so lucky. They hadn't gotten three steps up the rocks before Frank and Hans grabbed them by their boots and pulled them back down.

A second boom rocked the lakeside. Gravel skittered down the hill. As Mary pushed her pack inside the cave, dirt pelted her cap and shoulders. Outside, the brothers struggled helplessly against the stronger men.

"Stop!" Hans' voice echoed across the rocks. "Don't go! Not while they're blasting! Just give him the account book!"

"Listen to him, girl!" Solomon yelled while holstering his pistol and starting up the bank after Mary.

"I won't give it back!" Mary yelled. "It proves you're a crook!"

Solomon stopped climbing for a second and smiled broadly. Then with a burst of motion, he lept and reached up for her boot.

Mary pulled her leg up just in time. His fingers brushed across her heel.

Argh! How Mary hated that man and his smile! She spun on her knees, grabbed a handful of mud and threw it into his upturned face.

She backed farther into the cave before climbing to her feet. Solomon's head and neck came level with the entrance of the cave. Wiping the mud from his face, his evil smile suddenly returned.

A smile? Why? She was out of his reach.

Without warning, a third, even louder boom shook the cave. Mary stumbled backward down the corridor. Dirt and rocks broke loose from the ceiling.

Then, to her horror, the narrow opening and Solomon's smirking face disappeared as the corridor collapsed in front of her. The rumbling ended only a few seconds after it began.

Mary sat on the cave floor, legs straight out with her arms wrapped tightly around her pack. Mud caked her face and arms.

But the mud didn't concern her, or the pain from landing hard on the cave floor.

What bothered her was the silent blackness.

Trapped!

Mary lowered her face to her pack and cried.

CHAPTER 14

DELIVERANCE

For several minutes, Mary sat in the inky darkness and let her tears flow.

Now she knew why Solomon had smiled. He knew exactly how many gunpowder blasts had been planned. All he had to do was chase her into the cave and wait for the third blast to bury her alive–and the evidence of his crimes along with her. And what Solomon would do with Tom and Billy, Mary feared to guess.

Her hand slid down her pack. As it slid, she felt cool glass against her fingertips. She ran her hands over the metal, invisible in the pitch darkness though it was merely inches from her face.

The lantern? Of course! Like an igniting wick, her mind's eye suddenly visualized the lantern strapped to the side of her pack.

"Yes!" she cried aloud. She fumbled with the straps. She didn't need to see—she'd lit a lantern in the dark plenty of times!

Moments later, yellow light pushed away the darkness. A dense wall of rock and dirt completely blocked the corridor to the lake. It was a miracle she hadn't been crushed.

Now all she had to do was follow the corridor to the stream, then follow the stream to the wall of gold and crystal!

Unless she ran into the bear. That would bring a sudden end to her escape. Hopefully, she would exit the caves just as she and

Tom and Billy had the other day. And if Solomon and Frank were waiting for her—it didn't matter.

Mary swallowed hard. Better to be caught and alive than to be trapped and left to die in the cave!

Summoning courage, Mary lifted her lantern and headed down the corridor, listening for any signs of the bear. But she heard only the scuff of her boots and trickling water. She passed the incline where they'd seen the bear and where the old bone still lay on the floor. Grinning confidently, she turned left at the T.

Confidence rising, she pressed on, but as she entered the corridor, lantern light reflecting off water brought her abruptly to a halt.

The sloping cave floor where the bear had driven them into the stream was completely flooded. Mary couldn't even see the original stream, so high was the waterline.

A cold realization swept over her.

"No way out . . . " The words spilled slowly from her suddenly trembling lips. For a second, she thought about diving into the icy water, but then backed away. She would surely drown.

Mary turned and walked toward the main chamber. As she reached the T, lantern light glared off undisturbed layers of spider webs. The webs blocked the right-hand corridor that neither she, Tom nor Billy had explored.

She picked up the old gnawed bone, using it to clear the cobwebs out of her way. As she rounded a corner, the lantern's yellow light rapidly filled a large circular chamber.

Mary raised her hand toward her mouth and gasped.

For a brief second, she stared at the outstretched claws of a brown bear. Her heart slowed its racing when she saw the wooden pole supporting the drooping and lifeless skin.

Mary's gaze moved from the bear into the chamber. Along its

circular walls, other animals hung suspended on wooden poles: a deer, a coyote, a mountain lion, and even an eagle. In the center of the room, flat stones ringed a fire's ashen remains.

A ring of animal skins? A fire? Here?

Making a guess, Mary quickly extinguished her lantern. She needed to save the little oil she had left, anyway.

The chamber plunged into darkness, but not an inky blackness as before. As minutes passed, her eyes adjusted, and a circle of gray light appeared above her in the center of the ceiling.

Yes! The chamber rose and formed a natural chimney—overgrown by brambles above, but still an opening—a way out!

Mary slowly paced around the stone room. Though her sight increased with every step, her hope began to fade. The chamber was shaped like a bottle—wider at the base and narrow at the top. The smooth walls could not be climbed!

For the second time, coldness settled over her. Deeper, more final, like being lost on a mountain trail in a blizzard. At one end, ten to fifteen feet of densely packed rock and dirt blocked the entrance to the cave. At the other end, a watery grave.

And directly above was her salvation, but far beyond her reach.

Mary lowered herself onto one of the flat stones by the fire pit. She removed her poncho and pack, staring into the ashes. As she did, she suddenly realized what this chamber might be.

The animal skins and the fire pit—hadn't her father told her these were Maidu burial grounds? Maybe this chamber had something to do with the passing of the dead, or even a mourning ceremony.

The dead! Mary shivered, then spun around on the stone.

She spread out her poncho, then lay flat on her back. She folded her arms behind her head and stared up at the gray opening. Tears sprang from her eyes, streaking her cheeks. Her thoughts wandered as the long day passed into evening, the bright blue opening above her slowly darkening to a deep gray.

Now, lying in the darkness, her heart broke. She thought how her parents would agonize over her disappearance, and later, even more over her death. No one would ever learn about Solomon's doctored account book because she had it in her pack! And worst of all, she had surely jeopardized Tom's and Billy's lives.

Mary could not deny it. It was her stubborn will and la fiebre del oro that finally brought her here, to this chamber ringed by animal skins, a place of mourning for the dead.

Mourning for the dead. Animal skins. Old insights stabbed her heart in a way that they had not done in a long, long time.

The Maidu, like many other tribes, understood God only through his creation. Through what they could admire or even fear, often in animals like the bear, the coyote, the mountain lion. That's why her father came west, to be a messenger of good news to the native tribes of California. To help them learn the truth about the One who is greater than creation, the Creator!

How many Maidu deaths had been mourned here? How many Maidu, for tens of centuries, had died without genuine hope, without faith in the one true God? And now, how many more of the peaceful Maidu would die without a saving faith because of her failures?

Where your treasure is, there will your heart be also, echoed her father's gentle voice.

Mary cupped her hands over her face and nodded. Was she any different than the Maidu who didn't know God—putting her desire in created things rather than her Creator?

Gold is friend to no man. Do not trust it! For what does it profit you, to gain the whole world but lose your own soul? whispered Ignácio's warning.

Mary squeezed her eyes shut in the blackness.

"Father, please forgive me," she cried. "I'm sorry I didn't trust you. I've had the gold fever too, and now I've ruined everything."

Then, as if God himself replied, a thunderous boom shook the cave floor. Mary bolted upright. But unlike the gunpowder blasts, the thunder and shaking continued, growing louder every second.

Mary groped around and found the lantern. Her shaking fingers quickly brought it to life. As yellow light bathed the circular chamber and its animal guests, a whistling roar suddenly reached her ears.

By the time she pushed herself to her feet, a head-high wall of foaming white water swept around the corridor into the room, spilling wildly across the chamber floor.

By the time Mary had lifted the lantern above her head, the swiftly rising water swirled around her waist. She had no time to grab her pack or poncho. No time to figure out what had happened.

Mary kicked her feet beneath the roiling water. She felt herself quickly rise as she struggled to hold the lantern above the currents that slapped her face. The mounting water swept the animal skins and wooden poles upward around her as the mad whistling ended abruptly. The corridor leading into the chamber had completely disappeared underwater!

Mary kicked and kicked, spitting out water and straining to keep the lantern above the waterline, fighting to stay in the middle of the chimney beneath the gray opening.

Then, like soda water bubbling out of a bottle neck, the water spurted out the opening, pushing Mary through the stinging brambles onto a narrow stone slope.

For a second, as water enveloped her, Mary witnessed a most fantastic scene. The sky was nearly black, except for a band of stars and a full moon in the direction of Midas. Down to her left, the waterfall raged three times its original size. Tall beams of wood spewed over the falls and into the lake, borne away by floodwaters.

As Mary finally realized that the dam had burst, two wooden poles and a bearskin popped out the top of the chimney behind her.

One pole knocked the lantern from her hand; the other struck her in the back, knocking her forward. With a scream that was lost in the roar of the flood, Mary scrabbled at the soaked bearskin.

Eyes wide and bulging, she grabbed hold of the bear's head. Then, legs dangling in thin air, she disappeared over the rocky ledge.

CHAPTER 15

FLOOD

For one long terrifying moment, as Mary plummeted down the outside of the stone chimney, she thought she was going to die.

But the chimney from which she fell sloped beneath her, widening at the base. Belly flopping on the bearskin, air burst from her mouth as she clung with all her strength to its furry head.

Water spurting out of the chimney raced downward too, creating a fast-moving cushion that lifted the bearskin and Mary from the rocky slope.

With a scream caught in her throat, Mary watched as she dropped away from the chimney. Then, a hard bounce, and she was airborne again. The bearskin ripped from her hands as she struck the water. Down she plunged beneath the waves; then, clawing upward, she broke the surface.

Even as she gasped for breath, something massive pushed upward under her feet. Out of the water she rose with a tree trunk beneath her. Grasping for balance amid choppy waves, she caught hold of a thick limb, clasping her hands around it. She pulled herself tight to the tree, with her shoulders and head above water.

As she sped along the shoreline, Mary could tell that the

floodwaters had already swept the tree more than halfway down the lake—but not the lake as she had known it. The dam had emptied its bottled-up waters on top of a lake already full. Her lean-to, her looking glass and all of her precious possessions—gone, swept away downstream ahead of her.

Downstream—

The frightening thought barely completed itself when the tree bounced over a series of boulders, angled down and shot over the ravine—the ravine where Mary had first staked her claim! The momentum tossed her forward, wedging her waist between the limb and trunk and knocking the air from her lungs.

For a terrifying moment, Mary was unable to breathe as the tree fired through a curling tube of water. Then the tree dropped again, twisting sideways before righting itself in the white fury of the river. Ahead, the North Fork raced sharply around a bend to the left on its way to Midas.

Mary knew that she couldn't ride the tree forever. At any second, the tree could roll or flip, pitching her to her death on the rocks or beneath the waves.

As the tree hurtled toward the bend, Mary pulled herself up, bracing her knee in the Y of a limb. Her eyes scoured the riverside, so different-looking in the floodwaters at night!

Then the walls of the bend rose to meet her. And a hundred feet beyond the muddy curve, what had looked like a dozen small rocks seconds ago were now looming boulders— boulders bigger than she was tall! And in that moment, Mary knew that Death awaited her, with open arms of frothy white waves and a bosom of jagged stone.

In the same instant, dark streaks on the pale hillside also revealed their true forms. Thick tree roots dangled out from the cliff face, brushing along the top of the racing currents.

With no time to think but only to act, Mary pushed herself

halfway to her feet and leapt, arms reaching out.

She clasped her hands around one of the roots and hung on, her body swaying just above the waves. Digging her boots into the muddy cliff, her arms strained as she struggled upward.

A loud crack amid the roar of the flood caused Mary to glance downstream. Her tree bounced madly over the boulders at the edge of the river, snapping like a twig and flung end over end into the air by monstrous waves.

Hand over hand, Mary slowly pulled herself up the root. Finally, she found herself on her knees at the top of the bank. Staggering to her feet, Mary wiped mud from her eyes and face.

Unexpectedly, she discovered she was standing on a familiar rocky path.

Her clothes still plastered with mud and dripping with water, Mary lifted her head. Midas was only several hundred yards away. Slivers of moonlight glittered over an eerie watery landscape.

Midas?

Mary trudged forward, disbelieving. She started running toward the town, despite the throbbing pain in her side and her knee.

Only the upper half of Midas remained. The lower street, the stable, a hotel, the emporium, two houses, and the Chinese laundry—all gone! The rising North Fork had reached the middle tier of buildings—Solomon's buildings! What had happened to the shop owners and townspeople? And Tent Town across the river had become a plastered quilt of alternating light and dark squares. Miners scrambled for higher ground.

Mary looked back to the flooding street. She had to find out if Tom and Billy had somehow escaped Solomon's clutches—

and the flood. And what of Carolina and her family?

As she ran, rain began to fall. Not a gentle rain, but large, splattering drops. Despite the dark clouds that threatened to choke the full moon and the sheets of rain stinging her face, hope flared brightly in her heart. If the Lord could deliver her from the cave and a death-defying ride down the angry river, He could surely save her friends.

Out of breath, Mary limped to a halt in the street near Solomon's Store. To the left, the rising floodwaters crept slowly but steadily up the hill toward the Intelligence Office. A dozen townspeople and shop owners struggled up the muddy street with sacks flung over their backs, or crates clutched to their chests. Among them was the old Chinese couple who had owned the laundry! More voices called down from the dark street above. A woman screamed, and a child was crying.

Then, in answer to her unspoken prayer, the door to Solomon's Store flung open. With the glow of lantern light behind them, Tom and Billy appeared, with Frank right behind. He clutched the scruff of their shirts. With a growl, he shoved the boys into the street. As the rain flattened his groomed hair, Frank planted his hands on his hips and watched the brothers regain their balance.

"Thank you, God!" Mary cried, breaking into a run. "Tom! Billy!"

The brothers looked up, stunned but grinning wildly.

As she hugged them, over their shoulders she saw Solomon lugging a heavy crate and staggering out of the store.

Solomon saw Mary at once. He froze, dropping the crate. Clenching his fists, his face twisted into a crazed snarl as he stomped toward her through the mud.

Mary held her ground and met his gaze straight on. She would not back down. Not now, even though she no longer had the account book as evidence against him.

Crack! Then booming snaps! Sounds like cannon blasts spun Mary and the brothers around.

She knew the sounds.

"Run!" Mary shouted, tearing her gaze from the rushing river and pushing Tom and Billy uphill. Wide-eyed, Solomon and Frank ran too, legs pumping through the mud.

The cracking, snapping, breaking sounds deafened them.

A wall of broken and tumbling beams came rushing around the bend. The collapsing dam had completely given way, firing its largest timbers downstream, collecting flotsam on the way. But its momentum was so great the turn of the river bank could not contain the raging flow.

The massive wall kept its speed and direction and rolled into Solomon's hotel and store with the force of a dozen steam engines.

The explosion of water and flying timbers twenty feet long completely flattened Solomon's buildings as it swept by. Only a few scattered pieces of framing lumber, shredded calico, and clothing were left in its wake. Another wave of water surged up the street, lapping over Solomon's and Frank's boots before retreating into the swollen river.

Solomon turned and collapsed to his hands and knees. Screaming at the top of his lungs, he pounded his fists in the mud.

"My gold! All my gold!"

Mary walked slowly to his side, her voice trembling as she spoke.

"Solomon, gold is friend to no man. And you should've built your house on rock instead of sand!"

Then Mary's face grew deadly serious. "But you and Frank shouldn't be worrying about where your gold went to. Men hang by the neck for far less than what you two've done. I'd be on my way out of town, and fast."

Still on his hands and knees, Solomon looked up, his face splattered with mud. He glanced nervously at Frank; then, without a word, he scrambled to his feet and started sprinting up the hill.

As the two men retreated into the darkness, Mary noticed Carolina, the twins Isabel and Ramón, and a lantern-toting Julio hurrying down the street.

"Mary! Mary!" Carolina cried out, "What should we do? The river, it keeps rising!"

Mary smiled and pointed upward, her heart beating rapidly with a confidence that beamed through her tears.

Her father's lantern shimmered like a star, faithful and true, giving light for all to see, pointing the way to safety.

And home!

CHAPTER 16

HOME

Mary Muhlenberg leaned forward on her knees and tightly gripped her spade with both hands. She angled the metal blade toward the gravelly soil in front of her.

She ignored the stinging streams of sweat dripping into her eyes from her auburn hair and dusty forehead. She ignored the shadows of her father and another man cast by the noonday sun.

She had a posthole to dig, and a stubborn rock was not going to stop her!

"Mary," her father chided jokingly, "that hole can wait."

She blew a wisp of hair from her face and looked up over one shoulder. Her lips, still pressed tightly together from her struggle with the unmoving rock, opened into a wide smile.

"Ignácio!" she exclaimed, dropping the spade. She jumped to her feet and brushed the dirt from her corduroys.

The finely dressed ranchero bowed as he removed his felt hat. He gestured with a hand toward the freshly painted church building behind him.

"Mary, it is so good to see you working with your father," the ranchero said through a wide smile of his own.

The gleaming white walls, gray tin roof and tall steeple contrasted brightly against the blue autumn sky. Sunlight reflected off the three windowpanes facing the crest of the hill. Tom, Billy and two other men held cans of white paint and brushed the finishing touches on the entrance hall and front steps. One of the men was Julio, Ignácio's brother-in-law.

"My sister was right," the ranchero continued. "It appears that the townspeople have been most helpful. And your father says you worked as hard as anyone."

"Three days," Mary said, her eyes beaming. "We'll have the church completely finished in just three days—can you believe it?"

"After watching how wholeheartedly you and your friends put yourselves into the Lord's work," Ignácio said with a wry grin, "I have no doubts at all, Señorita!"

Peter slipped his arm around Mary's shoulder and hugged her.

"How long will you be in town?" Mary asked Ignácio.

"For a week or two. I brought some of my vaqueros—or how do you say, 'cowhands'—with me, to help my sister and her husband rebuild their hotel."

Ignácio glanced quickly at Peter, then back to Mary.

"As you know, since I run one of the oldest ranchos along the Feather River, I hear many rumors. These rumors come from many places: businessmen in San Francisco, Sacramento, Nevada City. And of course, I listen to rumors when I sell my beef in towns like Midas, Poverty Hill and Whiskey Flat.

"But on rare occasions, I will hear a story from Maidu, Yana or Nisenan headmen. One occasion was but two days ago, as I made my way here to Midas."

The ranchero's eyes twinkled.

"This is the essence of the story: that a certain, nearby lake was restored to those who have always dwelled on its shores, and how cowardly thieves were put to flight by a brave young woman.

"So now I ask, did not God miraculously reward that brave young woman? Though perhaps in an unexpected way."

Mary bent over and picked up her spade.

"Excuse me," she said, joy dancing suddenly in her eyes. She tapped the warm metal blade against an open palm, "but I really should get back to work."

With a smile beaming brighter than pure gold, she dropped to her knees and resumed digging.

Check out the *Tom Jefferson Mystery* series...

Book 1

"Tom Jefferson like you have never seen him before!"
Will W., history lover, blogger.

CHAPTER 1

BLACKBEARD

"SNAKE EYES!"

Disbelieving, I sank back on my heels and stared at the motionless dice: my third unlucky toss in a row.

Digging into my waistcoat pocket for another half-shilling, I found only silk lining. Hazard, the game my friends and I were playing, had emptied my purse again.

"Unlucky toss, Will," Jack consoled, echoing my thoughts. Beneath the glow of oil lanterns, the blacksmith's apprentice snatched up the painted wooden cubes and his winnings.

Jack rattled the dice in his palm. "Another wager, anyone?"

Kneeling in the dusty yard behind the Forge and Hammer blacksmith shop, my fellow gamblers shook their heads. The fading July sunset streaked the horizon with layers of ruby and magenta.

"Jack Curly, you've cleaned us out." Fifteen-year-old Thomas Jefferson tipped back his tricorn, revealing his sandy-red hair. Freckles arced his nose and cheekbones. Tom and I had become fast friends, perhaps because we both lost our fathers the year before.

Fellow students Ben and Sam, a year younger than Jefferson and I, shook their heads. The husky twins grabbed their three-cornered hats from a fencepost and dusted off their indigo and maroon silk coats and cream breeches.

The blacksmith's apprentice grinned. He clinked the coins into a hand-painted glass bowl detailing scenes of pirates and treasure chests. Jack created the bowl during his first apprenticeship with a glassblower in Jamestown.

"Your credit's good, Will Blair," Jack offered. "Gentlemen honor their debts."

I laughed. "A gentleman? In name only. I live with a kind and generous uncle. But without an inheritance, I must distinguish myself."

"Join the militia and fight the French!" Sam offered, brandishing an imaginary sword.

Ben wagged a finger. "I've one better. Find a rich widow like Colonel George Washington did." He reached out as if accepting Martha Custis' hand for a waltz.

I glanced at Jack. His mouth twisted slightly. A smirk? A frustrated smile? I understood. Craftsmen rarely became gentlemen. Skill meant little — only your station in life, and money — and lots of it.

"Serve the Colonies," Jefferson said, his eyes serious. "As a newly elected burgess, Colonel Washington will use his position to help secure our representation with the British Parliament."

Jack smiled slyly as he slipped the dice into a pocket behind his leather apron. "Whatever you do, keep quiet about our games. Wouldn't want anyone expelled, would we?"

I shuffled my feet. Getting expelled from grammar school for gambling would be disastrous. Next month I would turn 16, leave the Grammar School behind and enroll in the School of Philosophy at William and Mary. My education was crucial to being accepted as a gentleman — and gaining the freedom to do whatever I chose with my time and money.

I scratched my head, then tucked my braid back beneath my tricorn. One expense was unavoidable. Whether gentry or middling class, I'd soon be expected to wear an itchy wig — grizzled gray if my budget could afford one.

A jovial voice rumbled from the forge behind us.

"Finished, lads?"

Seth Beaufort, the barrel-chested blacksmith and owner of the Forge and Hammer, strode into the yard. He yanked off leather gloves, then brushed layers of coal dust from his swarthy face and black bushy beard.

"Night and trouble beckon," he warned, waving a big hand. "Surely you've heard the rumors?"

Ben's eyes widened. "About the ghosts? That Blackbeard and his crew have returned from their graves?"

Jack stood up, treasure bowl in hand. "Fact is, forty years ago, Williamsburg's General Court convicted Blackbeard's crew of piracy. Thirteen of them, mind you. Hanged them just north of town, by the gully."

"Thirteen. . ." Sam muttered shakily.

Jack lifted his chin and pulled on an imaginary noose, his mouth twisting into a ghastly O.

"What happened to Blackbeard?" Ben asked.

The smithy chuckled, his teeth a crescent moon peeking through storm clouds.

"When the British captured his flagship, it took 25 pistol and musket shots and a knife to drop him. A British Lieutenant lopped off his head. Then, upon returning to port, stuck it on a pole at the river entrance to Norfolk. Several years later, a silversmith brought Blackbeard's skull to Williamsburg, plated it with silver, and made it into a punch bowl!"

"Naw!" Sam grimaced.

"It's true," Jack added, leaning in, his voice dark and mysterious. "That bowl's been hidden in the Raleigh Tavern ever since. Now, Blackbeard's crew have come back and claim their captain's skull and return it to him!"

"And haunt the families of those who sentenced them to hang!" the smithy added approvingly.

Jefferson barked a laugh, breaking the spell. "Ghosts? I don't believe a word of it."

"But folks have seen 'em," Jack argued. "Floating shapes in tattered robes and pirate shirts, bandanas wrapped 'round their heads. Some with eye patches, some swords, and some toting sacks for plunder and the silver skull!"

"Eye patches!" Jefferson rolled his eyes. "Now, that's original."

"Mock if you must," Jack said, straightening, "but Matthew the Tinsmith wouldn't lie. Mr. Sedwick, who works for the Virginia Gazette, is as honest as they get! And that's just naming two."

Jefferson crossed his arms. "They're honest, I grant you. They saw something, but ghosts? I won't accept that notion and neither should you."

A stupid idea burst into my head. And unfortunately, it escaped from my mouth before I could stop it.

Ben and Sam backed up a step, jaws dropping.

Seth and Jack swapped worried glances, their faces glum.

Jefferson simply smiled.

"Catch the ghosts — why didn't I think of that myself? Will, you're brilliant, simply brilliant!"

The following noon, I leapt down from the Wren Building's front steps, Latin and Greek lesson books in hand. Classmates from the William and Mary Grammar School jostled past me, racing the mile-long Duke of Gloucester Street for the choicest spots to view the public branding.

Across town, near the Capitol where the House of Burgesses met, the Public Gaol housed criminals and other law-breakers. While missing church too often might land you hand and foot in the stocks, not paying your debts could make the cold, damp jail cells of Williamsburg's oldest building your home until your creditors were satisfied. But for theft, the penalty could be permanent: having a T branded into your palm.

The crowds swelled, gentry in breeches and waistcoats of silk, satin, and fine linen, with stockings, buckled shoes, and powdered wigs. Tradesmen and craftsmen in their middling wools. And slaves, in their loose-fitting trousers, makeshift shirts, and floppy-brimmed hats.

Jefferson's red hair made him easy to spot. As I approached, he drew a sheaf of papers trapped between the pages of a book by the Roman philosopher Cicero, his favorite classical thinker.

"I spent the last hour with your Dr. Small. He is a treasure trove of knowledge about Williamsburg's history. I believe I shall enjoy sitting under him when I enter the College in the spring."

I grinned. Dr. William Small, a professor of mathematics and philosophy at William and Mary, often invited me to join him at Charlton's coffee house near the Capitol and merchant exchange. Why he took an interest in me, I wasn't sure. Perhaps my uncle had put in a good word. Regardless, I knew that Tom would enjoy meeting the wise doctor, and Dr. Small, a bookish bachelor from Scotland, would equally enjoy Tom.

Tom's voice brimmed with excitement. "He gave me the names of the court officials who sentenced Blackbeard's crew to hang, plus a list of those officials' descendants still living in Williamsburg. Then I found out which homes and businesses had been visited by the ghosts and what items were reported stolen."

"Hmm. . ." I studied the list. "Good pirate treasure —jewelry and coins or items fashioned of gold or silver."

Jefferson nodded, pointing at the list. "There's only one family remaining the ghosts haven't visited. Notice anything?"

I looked again, top to bottom. Understanding flooded me like a lantern dispelling shadows.

I grinned. "Our ghosts visited these families in alphabetical order!"

"Too much intelligence for former pirates, eh?" Jefferson's eyes sparkled. "And being smart ghosts, I think they'll strike tonight — before the moon waxes any brighter."

"So, we're off to catch our ghosts?" I drew a deep breath.

Jefferson nodded, folding the papers and turning toward the Gaol. "Now, let's see what's going to happen to that unfortunate fellow who stole the magistrate's horse."

The gibbous moon played hide and seek with a swath of clouds drifting lazily across the night sky. Behind us a windmill slowly creaked, turning with the breeze. The gurgling, black stream flashed silver whenever moonlight reflected along its rushing surface.

Jefferson and I silently passed through a field of chest-high grass behind the cabinetmaker's house toward Botetourt Street. If Jefferson's reasoning was correct, we might catch our ghosts. Not really catch — just follow them to their hideout and then seek help.

The last house on Jefferson's list loomed fifty yards ahead. To our left rose the black silhouette of a barn, two outbuildings, and a necessary bordered by a cornfield. To the right, a two-story home with two fireplaces at each end. And ahead, a small rise crowned by an old weeping willow.

Jefferson and I darted from the high grass to the tree. The breeze coursed noisily through its swaying limbs, masking our approach. The rustling leaves, coupled with the chorus of nearby crickets, covered our whispered conversation as we knelt in the deep shade beside the willow's trunk.

"Tom, what if they're really ghosts?" I asked.

Jefferson sighed. "Well, I suppose that Devilsburg will attract even larger crowds willing to empty their purses on another unexplained occurrence. Aside from the stolen goods, someone will turn this story into a handsome profit."

"Devils-burg?" I asked, not understanding.

A smile gleamed faintly on Tom's face.

"Williamsburg has so many distractions. You've seen the motto above the mantle at the Apollo Tavern — *hilaritas sapitentiae et bonae vitae proles*. That's Latin for 'jollity, offspring of wisdom and good living.' Now that I'm 16 and soon to start college, no more tempting afternoons of Hazard. No more wasted evenings with lads at the coffeehouse. No late nights chasing ghost pirates. Just my studies, even if it takes 15 hours a day."

Jefferson crossed his arms over a knee, his voice suddenly wistful.

"Will, the Almighty didn't give us liberty to spend on our pleasures. The Colonies need gentlemen like Colonel Washington and Dr. Small — men who will make sacrifices and take a stand for what's important."

The darkness hid my reddening cheeks. Gentlemen and sacrifices? Liberty? I knew I didn't share Tom's noble ideals. My embarrassment was cut short as he gripped my forearm.

"Something's moving!" he hissed.

Yes, something lumbered slowly from the cornfield toward the barn before stopping abruptly. The dark, misshapen figure stood but a stone's throw away.

I fought down the fear that urged me to run.

"Doesn't look like a ghost," Jefferson whispered, craning forward.

"Or a pirate," I added, peering through the waving limbs as the breeze picked up. How strange! The shape had boxlike angles.

Jefferson wrinkled his nose. "What's that?"

I sniffed the air. Something acrid, like. . .

"Sulfur?" he suggested.

I nodded.

A tiny light flickered within the dark shape. I started to point, but froze, as cold and motionless as marble.

There, by the barn, floated three ghostly pirates, just like Jack had described! Heads wrapped in dark bandanas. Black eye patches and pale swords. Tattered shirts and cloaks of muted purples and scarlet. Large gray sacks slung over their shoulders.

But to my greater shock, Jefferson leapt to his feet. Without explanation he darted from beneath the willow.

"Yaaa!" he screamed, arms waving.

In the same instant I heard a loud thud.

The ghost pirates vanished — and the barn became a dark silhouette once again.

"Tom!" His name raggedly burst from my lips as I sprang up and plunged after him. My faculties finally caught up with my pumping arms and legs when I reached the spot where the misshapen figure had once stood.

But Tom was nowhere to be seen.

I started searching the ground for footprints when moonlight glinted off an object at my feet.

I bent down and picked up a smooth, translucent rectangle. Broken glass? But before I could examine it, Jefferson's shout interrupted the night once again.

Slipping the object into a pocket, I headed in the direction of the shout.

Three steps later, a dark shape appeared suddenly from behind the corner of the barn and blocked my path.

I stumbled, fell to my knees before mammoth, booted feet. I stared upward at the huge man looming over me, if a man he really was.

The giant wore loose-fitting breeches, girded by a wide belt that supported two shimmering cutlasses, one on each hip. A dark coat crossed with bandoleers stuffed with knives and pistols guided my disbelieving eyes to a broad face framed by black, tangled hair and a beard twisted into pigtails as thick as fingers.

For a second time, a smell like sulfur filled the air, followed by a red-orange flash that nearly blinded me.

Nearly.

I threw up my hands before my face. A ring of fire encircled the menacing head. His face glowed like pulsing embers.

His threatening eyes bored into mine.

"Blackbeard?" I croaked, unable to move my arms or legs. The starry sky spun round and round as I fell back, like a toppled tree.

The pirate laughed, long and hard. His deep voice rumbled through the flickering ring of flames, carried by the gusting wind into the darkness.

Check out the *Batter Up!* series...

Book 1

"Your stories are awesome!"
D. B., home schooling mother of four

①
GAME OVER

CHARLIE planted his left foot in the back corner of the batter's box and cut the air with a couple of practice swings. He lifted his head and stared down Benny Jones, the Cincinnati Gas Redlegs' big right-handed hurler.

Benny leaned forward and stared back, his eyebrows furrowing in concentration.

He'd already struck out 10 of Charlie's teammates, but not Charlie.

Not today, anyway.

As Benny straightened up on the pitcher's mound, Charlie's eyes surveyed the outfield.

Bottom of the seventh. Three runs down. Two outs. Bases loaded. If Charlie made an out the game would be over and Charlie's team, the Clifton Landing Red Stockings, named after the greatest base ball team in the whole U. S. of A., would not only lose the game, 9-6, but would fall into 2nd place behind the Redlegs with only two weeks left in the season!

The Redlegs' carrot-haired first baseman clapped his calloused bare hands together and shouted encouragement to his pitcher. "That big red C on his chest don't stand for Cincinnati—it stands for *chicken*! He ain't got no hits. Zip it past him!"

Charlie ignored the taunt though it was true. In the first inning he grounded out to the second baseman. In the third, flied out to the centerfielder. And in the fifth, walked on three straight pitches after Benny refused to obey the umpire and throw strikes. Charlie then scored a run on a two-bagger by his best friend, and fastest Red Stocking, Luther Robinson.

Benny's arm snapped forward like a slingshot.

The base runners started moving, but Charlie never took his eyes off the ball.

Gritting his teeth, Charlie brought his bat down and around in a swift smooth arc.

The clean crack of the bat split the air.

Charlie dropped his bat and watched.

Benny spun on a heel and stared toward deep left center, his hands hanging loose at his sides.

The ball climbed and climbed as the center fielder pedaled back, back.

Charlie started trotting toward first base as his teammate from third streaked across home plate.

Off to his right, Charlie heard Luther screaming at the top of his lungs, "A four-bagger! Charlie you did it – a *four*-bagger!"

But the centerfielder seemed to have a bead on the ball as he continued to back up, bare hands raised over his head, until he collided with the tall hedge and dense shrubs separating the ball field from Old Man Clifton's place.

Rounding first, Charlie could hardly believe it as the centerfielder's outstretched right hand snagged the arcing ball – when both player and ball disappeared into the hedge!

Seconds later he emerged from the dense green wall, pieces of brush caught in his hair, his arm raised high above his head.

With base ball in hand.

Stunned, Charlie stopped at second base.

Richard Hurly, the game's guest umpire and a professional

utility infielder for the *real* Cincinnati Red Stockings, leapt from behind the umpire's table in foul territory between home plate and first base, knocking and spilling the pitcher of fresh lemonade over the plate of tea cakes that Luther's mom had kindly provided.

The centerfielder waved his left arm wildly back and forth, displaying the ball.

The entire Redlegs' team danced out onto the field, clapping and cheering and stomping their feet.

Twenty-two-year-old Hurley tugged at his white Red Stockings uniform shirt with its large, fire-engine red C stitched on the front. He straightened his straw boater hat, drew back his shoulders, and after shooting Charlie a long disappointed look, called the game.

"Striker out! Redlegs 9, Red Stockings 6—game over!"

YOUNG HEROES

Enjoyable for readers of all ages.

Inspire the Hero!

YOUNG HEROES
ENJOYABLE FOR READERS OF ALL AGES

A TRAIL OF TEARS

CENTURY WAR # 1

DANIEL SWEETWATER is a 16-year-old Delaware Indian living with his preacher father among the Cherokee in 1838. They are forced to march with the Cherokee on a 1000-mile journey from Georgia to the Oklahoma Territory.

Cruel men and the daily pains of injustice hammer mercilessly at Daniel's faith in God. But God provides hope through a wise frontiersman and a missionary's courageous daughter. When unexpected tragedy comes, Daniel is faced with a choice. Will he follow a dark trail of vengeance? Or will he follow the light of truth and discover a special mercy hidden within his Christian heritage?

INVISIBLE EMPIRES

JOSIAH WASHINGTON, a 16-year-old former slave, longs to experience the true meaning of freedom in 1870's Philadelphia. Deeply hurt by the cruel injustices he has suffered, Josiah is unwittingly drawn into a convoluted plot to bring the Ku Klux Klan into the North.

When Josiah learns that he is but a small pawn in a much bigger and devious game, he must find a way to stop the KKK from igniting Philadelphia into a violent war of racial hatred.

Heroes and enemies spanning two generations collide, as God calls the past into account and brings evil men to justice.

CENTURY WAR # 2

Inspire the
Hero!

A City of Lies

CHRISTINE THOMPSON and ADAM VESTRY are reunited four years following their first adventure in *The Invisible Empire*. The year is 1876. Chicago, five years after the Great Fire, continues to rebuild its reputation as Queen of the West.

Christine, wanting to make her own way, joins a utopian community called New Eden, where new ideas, hard work and equality promise a recreated Paradise. Adam, an investigative reporter, pursues connections between organized crime and business. Following a trail of corruption to the doorstep of New Eden, Adam must find a way to rescue Christine and foil the evil that seeks to bring flames and destruction to Chicago once again!

CENTURY WAR # 3

Gold Rush!

MIDAS TOUCH # 1

MARY MUHLENBERG is an ambitious 16-year-old who joins the California Gold Rush in 1849. But despite her missionary father's warnings, she exchanges her Bible for a spade.

Touched by gold fever, Mary makes an ill-advised alliance with conniving entrepreneurs from Midas, a nearby mining town. Her escapades will threaten her father's work among the local tribes, compromise her faith and family, and imperil not only her life, but the lives of her friends.

When Mary finds herself trapped and alone, she is confronted by her poor judgment. She must face the darkness within herself. Only then will she be ready for the greatest test of her life.

YOUNG HEROES
ENJOYABLE FOR READERS OF ALL AGES

WRECKERS OF THE REEFS

STORIES TO INSPIRE

KIDNAPPED at birth by an evil uncle in 1879, Lucas escapes to freedom with the help of a kindly captain of a merchant ship. The ship goes down leaving Lucas clinging to the shattered mast, the lone survivor.

A"surfman," Abner Peake of the U.S. Life Saving Service, brings Lucas into his home. Now, Lucas dreams of becoming a surfman, like those brave men who rescued him.

Lucas must risk everything he has gained in a life or death rescue mission with the surfmen, leading to a surprising and life-changing discovery.

PONY EXPRESS PURSUIT

EXCITED by his new position as a Pony Express rider, 16-year-old Jack Bailey of Rainbow Ridge, Colorado, has no idea of a coming danger that will fall upon him and his community. Jack is tasked with receiving and delivering a very important document – the deed to a motherlode gold mine. But others know the document's worth and await a chance to steal it.

When Jack is drugged and his mail is stolen, will he rise up and rally the community? Will Jack finally prove that he is a man worthy of the title Pony Express Rider?

STORIES TO INSPIRE

INSPIRE THE HERO!

NEWSBOY EMPIRE

ORPHANED, Jimmy Small works as a newsboy near New York City's infamous Five Points in the summer of 1907. Sleeping in a garbage-littered alley, Jimmy awakens to find a young amnesiac boy named Philip sleeping next to him. They become fast friends and form a business partnership.

Philip is kidnapped by young thugs who believe he is the son of wealthy parents. Will a quarter dollar and a promise be enough for Jimmy to save his friend and business partner? Will the mystery of Philip's identity and Jimmy's dream of owning a newsstand ever be fulfilled?

STORIES TO INSPIRE

SAVED BY THE WIRELESS

STORIES TO INSPIRE

MYSTERIOUS messages haunt 16-year-old Tom Barnes as he works at his new telegraph station in the New England town of Rockley Cove in 1911. Nearly every day, the word "Donner" comes across the wire.

When the biggest storm of the season sweeps in along the coast, Tom picks up a distress signal from a passenger liner at sea—the Olivia. His friend Grace is aboard and Tom must act. He commandeers a hulking motorboat and sets out for the imperiled liner.

Amid the deadly, tossing waves, Tom's courage and resolve are tested and his hard-earned success hangs on every decision. Will they reach the Olivia in time? Can he find a way to save Grace and the others? Will he survive to solve the "Donner" mystery?

YOUNG HEROES
ENJOYABLE FOR READERS OF ALL AGES

TREACHERY ON THE GREAT LAKES

STORIES TO INSPIRE

ORPHANED in 1899 at the age of 14, apprentice longshoremen Nat Morton works on the Chicago docks but yearns to become a boat pilot. With a lost inheritance hanging over his head, Nat's lowly station in life provides him little hope.

A helpless figure flailing in the water creates an unexpected opportunity. Nat saves the *Jessie Drew*'s pilot and their friendship lands Nat behind the wheel in the pilot house.

A vicious storm with Nat at the wheel tests him to his core. Will he stay the course, save the ship, and the lives entrusted to him?

CALL OF THE PRAIRIE

BEHIND BARS in a New York City police station in 1904, 16-year-old Bob Chester ponders his bad luck. A menacing legal guardian and scheming con artists fuel Bob's dream of going west and becoming a cowboy. Released unexpectedly, he gathers the few dollars he has saved and flees New York for Oklahoma.

Working hard to prove himself as a ranch hand, Bob discovers a ruthless plot to steal his boss's property and holdings. Bob's character and wits will be tested to the utmost in a desperate race across the prairie to expose the plot and save his boss and new friend.

STORIES TO INSPIRE

INSPIRE THE HERO!

TRIAL BY FIRE

DISTRESSED by the failure of his town's bucket brigade to safely extinguish the fires plaguing Lakeville, 16-year-old high school student Jake Walters and his schoolmates create a volunteer fire company. It's 1903 and, during their summer vacation, the boys raise their own funds and purchase a used, water and hose pump wagon.

But a prominent citizen resists Jake's efforts, insisting that their bucket brigade is sufficient. When the town's biggest factory goes up in flames and a young girl is trapped inside the building, Jake must decide if he will risk his life and everything he has worked for when no one else steps up to rescue the girl.

STORIES TO INSPIRE

RACE FOR THE SKIES

STORIES TO INSPIRE

STRUGGLING to make his way, 15-year old Andy Nelson is a gifted mechanic in a 1910 Midwest town. He finds a customer's wallet, but his greedy boss, Seth Talbot, wants the money. Andy refuses, hoping to return the money to the customer. He banks the money and hides the empty wallet. This act defines the course of Andy's life and he is forced to flee the town

During his journeys, Andy helps an entrepreneur dislodge his biplane from a barn roof, striking up a friendship and a new job. When Andy learns to fly, he is entered in a great air race. But his past sneaks up on him when the greedy Talbot tracks him down to destroy his reputation and life.

Caught in a doubly dangerous race for the skies and the pursuit of justice, Andy's integrity and courage will be tried and tested as never before.

Young Heroes
More Great Stories

Ghost Pirates

TOM JEFFERSON MYSTERIES

WHEN a ghostly Blackbeard and his crew rise from the dead and begin haunting the people of Williamsburg, Virginia, young Tom Jefferson and his closest friend Will Blair set about to unravel the mystery.

Little do they realize the chain of events their bold actions will set into motion, events that will forever shape their lives, and the life of a fledgling nation.

This first book in the *Tom Jefferson Mystery* series gives readers a fresh and exciting look at one of America's storied characters and times.

Readers of all ages will enjoy this first book in the *Tom Jefferson Mystery* series.

I Love Baseball

SUMMER OF 1869 — the bustling riverfront city of Cincinnati, Ohio. Steamboats churn the Ohio River as the nation's ever-expanding economy thrives in the wake of the Civil War. Two 16-year-olds, Charlie Martin and his best friend Luther Robinson, love "base ball" and follow the exploits of America's first professional base ball team — the undefeated Cincinnati Red Stockings.

When a ruthless shipping magnate ends their dream for a Cincinnati Youth Club ball field, the two square off against one of Cincinnati's most powerful men, risking their honor, friendships and freedom to right a grievous wrong. Readers of all ages will enjoy this first book in the *Batter Up!* series.

BATTER UP! #1

DIVE
A LITTLE
DEEPER ...

CALIFORNIA OR BUST

Our journey through the desert was from Monday afternoon…until Thursday morning at sunrise. The weary journey last night, the mooing of the cows for water, their exhausted condition, with the cry of "Another ox down," the stopping of the [wagon] train to unyoke the poor dying beast to let him follow at will or stop by the wayside and die, and the weary tramp of man and beast, worn out with heat and famished for water, will never be erased from my memory …

49er Sally Hester, from *They Saw the Elephant*
by Jo Ann Levy

For many weeks we had been accustomed to see property abandoned and animals dead or dying. But those scenes here doubled and trebled. Horses, mules, and oxen, suffering from heat, thirst, and starvation, staggered along until they fell and died. Both sides of the road for miles were lined with dead animals and abandoned wagons. Around them were strewn with yokes, chains, harnesses, guns, tools, bedding, clothing, cooking-utensils, utensils, and many other articles, in utter confusion. The owners had left everything, except what they could carry on their backs, and hurried to save themselves.

49er Margaret Frink, from *They Saw the Elephant*

You may rest assured that I have an older head on my shoulders by about 1,000 years and when I left the states [for the California territory].

49er William Swain, from *The World Rushed In*
by J.S. Holliday

ADDITIONAL READING

California Gold Rush—Eye Witness Accounts

Holliday, J.S. *The World Rushed In, The California Gold Rush Experience*. New York: Simon and Schuster, 1981.

Levy, Jo Ann. *They Saw the Elephant, Women in the California Gold Rush*. Hamden, Connecticut: The Shoe String Press, 1990.

California Gold Rush General

Editors. *The Forty-Niners*. New York: Time-Life Books, 1974.

Ketchum, Lisa. *The Gold Rush, Companion Volume to the PBS. The West*. Boston: Little, Brown and Company, 1996.

Paul, Rodman W. *The California Gold Discovery, Sources, Documents, Accounts and Memoirs Relating to the Discovery of God at Sutter's Mill*. Georgetown, California: The Talisman Press: 1967.

Jackson, Donald Dale. *Gold Dust, the Saga of the Forty-Niners*. New York: Alfred A. Knopf, 1980.

Blumberg, Rhoda. *The Great American Gold Rush*. New York: Bradbury Press, 1989.

El Dorado

George, Philip Brandt, Administrative Editor. *The Search for El Dorado*. Alexandria, Virginia: Time-Life Books, 1994.

www.ingramcontent.com/pod-product-compliance
Lightning Source LLC
Chambersburg PA
CBHW070639130626

46555CB00006B/2609